The View from Nob Hill

Ty Hutchinson

Chapter One

Jill Pittman

I WAS ALONE, but not lonely—far from it. In fact, I was feeling giddy. It was Friday, my children were away for the night, my husband would arrive home soon, and I had just uncorked a bottle of Cabernet. Date night was off to a good start. I turned up the music on the portable speaker—Duran Duran—and danced around the living room while sipping the lovely red. I should have waited, but someone had to determine whether the wine I bought from Trader Joe's was a deal.

I was married to a wonderful man, Alan. I had two teenage children, Mia and Ollie. And I lived in a three-story house on Nob Hill with incredible views of the San Francisco Bay. As far as I was concerned, I was living my perfect life. This wouldn't be the case three days later.

Mia, my oldest at seventeen, was at a sleepover at a friend's house. Ollie, my sweet sixteen-year-old, was on a camping trip for the weekend. Once their plans were confirmed on Thursday, I told Alan that Friday would be our night. We hadn't had real alone time in ages, and the last time we had sex, it was quicker than a quickie. That night, there would be no fly-by sex or

1

shushing because the kids might hear us. I planned on singing an opera.

Unfortunately, a hiccup had developed Friday afternoon. VIP clients for Alan's company had come to town on short notice. He'd drawn the short straw and had to entertain them that evening. Not wanting to put a damper on what could still be a salvageable night, I had said, "Fine, just come home as soon as you can." It wasn't like we needed to be in bed by eleven.

Alan had had a lot of success early on in his career, and quickly made partner at a successful financial services firm in the city. With that success came a lot of responsibility. He had late nights and worked some weekends. There were client calls during dinner and, occasionally, a last-minute thing that screwed up our personal plans. But hey, that came with the territory, right? I couldn't complain. Alan provided a comfortable living for us. I was able to quit my job right after I had Ollie. Honestly, once I got a taste of this lifestyle, there was no returning to a dead-end nine-to-five.

Alan had texted me earlier to let me know that he and the clients would have dinner and maybe a couple of nightcaps before calling it a night. When eight o'clock rolled around, I sent him a text for an ETA. I still felt sexy in my dress and anticipated a lively night. The charcuterie board I had made still looked appetizing.

Alan was usually pretty good about answering me right away, so I was surprised when eight thirty rolled around and he hadn't responded. *Relax, Jill. He's probably listening to his client tell him a story and can't answer.*

I helped myself to another glass, knowing I couldn't keep that up all night without slurring my words. But hey, Alan was probably downing a couple of libations, too, so we'd both be primed to go when he got home.

Nine o'clock rolled around, and I still hadn't heard from

Alan. I'd actually thought he'd be home by that time. I checked my phone. The message I'd sent was still unread. *Maybe he read it on his lock screen.* I just thought he would have found a minute to type out a quick response in that hour's time. Nope.

However, the bottle I'd opened earlier was feeling light. I had a decision: either go stingy on the next pour or continue my streak, open another bottle, and run the risk of passing out on Alan. I glanced back at the clock. *It is only nine...* I might not have had the energy of a teenager, but I wasn't in the grave yet. I tried calling my friend Helen to pass the time, but she wasn't picking up.

About an hour later there was still no response, and I was officially annoyed. I fired off another text. *This is so not like him.* I was also a little worried—what if something happened? Had he been in an accident?

I called his cell, but there was no answer. He usually didn't like partying late, but these were important clients who were probably in the mood for more than a simple dinner. Still, I didn't want to give up hope on our date night. The earliest Mia would come home was noon on Saturday. Ollie wasn't due to return until Sunday night. We had no curfew, and we could sleep in.

Finally Alan responded with a blurred selfie of himself sitting next to two men. They were all holding drinks and had silly smiles on their faces. He said sorry and that he'd be home soon.

Accepting fate, I'd already gone through a bottle and a half, filling my glass to the rim with each pour. I'd gone from happy-tipsy to irritated-drunk. My fantasy of a kid-free night with Alan so we could act like a couple of teenagers ourselves was fading fast. The charcuterie board and I were both starting to look like tired messes.

Part of me wanted to scream into the phone, "What's taking

so long, Alan?!" I mean, come on. Can't you just tell them you have to go? I didn't think I was asking much, considering our plans for the night. Alan was just as excited about the evening as I was.

I decided to move the party to the balcony outside our bedroom. I headed up to the third floor with a glass in one hand and a bottle in the other. Mia's and Ollie's rooms were on the second floor, along with an entertainment room and a guest bedroom. The first floor housed a living room, a dining room, an office, and an open concept kitchen that led to a large deck.

When I hit the second-floor landing, I noticed a light coming from Ollie's bedroom. He'd left his desk lamp on. I switched it off, and just as I turned to go, I thought I heard something click. I turned around and spied Ollie's camera on his tripod. He had gotten into photography two years ago and had really come to like it. He already owned three cameras and had even started a photography club at school.

I tried twisting my bare foot against the carpet, thinking maybe I had made the noise, but it didn't quite sound the same.

You're just buzzed, Jill. Forget about it.

I continued up to our bedroom and walked out onto our balcony. I filled my glass and plopped down on a chair. I'd concluded that we would need to take a rain check on our date night. At the very least, I'd enjoyed some decent wine and got a little dance cardio in.

The weather that night was chilly but clear. The usual fog hadn't rolled in, so I had a fantastic view of the city and the bay. I drew a deep breath and admired the twinkling lights. It was a million-dollar view, nearly perfect—nearly. A thirty-two-story high-rise stood right in the middle of the view. It wasn't grouped together with other buildings to add to the skyline; it was an outlier. But it had been there for three decades by the time our house was built. I had nicknamed it the Middle Finger.

Its real name was the Residence, one of the city's first luxury high-rises. The architecture was dated, but it definitely had its charm. That didn't mean I liked it, though. In fact, it had been a major issue for Alan and me when we first considered buying the house. I'd fallen in love with the place the minute I set foot inside. Everything about it was perfect, except for the view from our bedroom. I told Alan the building was like a middle finger, telling us, "No, you can't have it all." Still, we bought the place, and I learned to live with it.

Alan was an amateur astronomer; he loved looking up at the stars and had a collection of costly telescopes. He'd left one of the lower-end models out on the balcony. I placed a hand on the railing to steady myself as I downed the rest of the wine in my glass. The width of the Middle Finger faced us dead on. If I looked through the telescope, I could see right into just about any apartment, as if I were standing outside with my nose to their window.

I peered through the eyepiece of the telescope and moved it around, scanning the building. I was surprised to see a number of people up so late doing all sorts of mundane things in their apartments with their drapes open and lights on. Some people were watching TV, one person was folding laundry, and another was doing push-ups. I continued to scan the apartments.

Wait, what was that?

I blinked my eyes for clarity, wobbling a bit. I might have had a bit more wine than I should have, and it was just a blip passing through the field of view, but...

Did I just see someone fall?

Chapter Two

Jill

It was a little after seven when I woke up the following morning. Alan lay next to me, breathing softly. He'd made it home in one piece, but I must have fallen asleep before he came home, because I had no recollection of talking to him or hearing him crawl into bed. Alan lay sprawled across the comforter. He'd removed his work shirt but still had one leg in his slacks. I had changed into my nightgown; I didn't remember doing it, though.

The room was brighter than usual, as only the sheer curtains were drawn closed, not the blackout. I noticed the sliding door to the balcony was open, and a slight draft was blowing into our room. A chill ran through my body. Alan must have gone outside before coming to bed. There was no way I would have gone to sleep with it open.

I swung my legs over the edge of the bed to sit up and felt a slight pounding in the front of my head. While I waited for the dizzy spell to pass, I noticed a scratch in my throat when I swallowed. I'd expected more damage, to be honest. I walked over to the balcony door and closed it. I didn't see my wine glass or the bottle anywhere.

Did I clean up, or did Alan?

I threw on a robe and washed my face quickly. On my way out of the bedroom, I pulled my husband's pants off his leg. He didn't stir. I checked the pants pockets and found his wallet, a few crumpled singles, and a receipt. Water spots on the receipt made it impossible to tell where it was from. I picked up the rest of his clothes and was a few steps from tossing it all into the hamper when I stopped short. I don't know why I did it—maybe it was his unusual behavior the night before—but I examined his shirt around the collar before bringing it up to my nose. I smelled Alan's cologne and nothing else.

Downstairs, in the kitchen, I washed down a couple of aspirin with a glass of cold water before I turned on the coffee maker. I couldn't wait until the whole pot was finished brewing; I moved the carafe and replaced it with my mug until it was full. I added milk and vanilla sweetener before taking a seat at the kitchen island.

I switched on the small TV in the kitchen to catch the morning news. A "breaking news" banner ran along the bottom of the screen with the name "Errol Tiller" written in block letters. Errol owned a successful advertising and PR agency in San Francisco. I'd met him a couple of times at fundraisers. He was known to be a generous man and seemed to always be involved with local charities. I turned the volume up.

The newscaster reported that Errol had fallen to his death from his penthouse suite at the Residence. My heart skipped a beat as the events of the previous night started to come back to me. *No, it couldn't have been... Did I see Errol fall to his death?*

I might have drunk a gallon of wine, but I would have remembered that. At least something like that. I would know if I'd seen someone fall, right? My thoughts reverted back to that moment. That blip I'd brushed off as a piece of dust in my eye

7

had really happened. I couldn't believe it. I actually saw someone fall from a building.

I leaned in closer to the television as the newscaster reported the cause of death was most likely suicide.

Suicide? I was shocked to hear that. Errol was always smiling and laughing when I encountered him.

I sat there, numb, as I watched the newscast. The anchorwoman said that calls to 911 had started coming in after 2:00 a.m. *Had I been up that late? And how much noise does a falling body make? Did it wake people up, or did people witness it? Maybe he was found later, already dead on the sidewalk.* The details surrounding his death were light. Most of the reporting was about Errol's life and his involvement in the community.

My experience with Errol was that he was a thoughtful and kind man. My daughter had spent the summer interning at his company and said she'd learned a lot about PR. Interning there had helped her to understand what it would be like to work in that field.

A feeling of sadness suddenly overcame me, as if I'd lost a close loved one. Which was weird, because my relationship with Errol hadn't been anything like that. We were associates at best; we only interacted if we happened to be at the same charity function. Alan had never even met the guy, even though he was a partner at a well-known financial firm and easily could have crossed paths with him in the business world. One year, Errol was named San Francisco's most eligible bachelor. Alan joked that *he* might have grabbed that spot had he not already been married. That was the only time I'd heard him mention Errol's name.

My cell phone chimed, and there was a notification for a calendar reminder. I'd forgotten that I had planned to meet a friend at the farmers' market later that morning. I guess waking up early with Alan still sleeping worked out for the best. I hurried upstairs, showered, and got ready. I left a note for Alan on the bedside table before kissing him on the forehead. I waited a moment for him to wake up and say goodbye. Nothing.

Chapter Three

SFPD

DETECTIVE PETE SOKOLOV worked homicide out of the Central Station in the North Beach neighborhood. The Residence stood near the corner of Stockton and Washington Streets, a mere ten-minute walk from the station. But Sokolov had been at his home in the Marina district when he received the early-morning call about a man falling out of the high-rise to his death. He arrived on the scene a little after 6:00 a.m. SFPD patrol cars were still parked to block traffic from traveling along Stockton. There were also a bunch of news vans parked nearby.

As he made his way to the front of the building, he quickly saw where the body had landed—it had caved in the top of a car. The medical examiner had already removed the body, but Sokolov didn't need to see it. CSI would have photos. Errol Tiller's death would be treated as a murder investigation until proven otherwise, but suicide seemed likely.

Detective Adrian Bennie, his partner, waved Sokolov over to where he stood, near the car. He had a cup of coffee in one hand, a cruller in the other, and a smile on his face. Bennie was always in a happy mood, no matter what. The same couldn't be said for Sokolov. It wasn't that he was always in a *bad* mood, just that he was Russian and doled out smiles sparingly. Next to Bennie was a patrol officer, who Sokolov assumed was first on the scene.

"You been here long?" Sokolov asked Bennie as he approached.

"Got here a few minutes before you. We just missed the body. This is Officer Delgado. He responded to the call."

"What do you know?" Sokolov asked Delgado.

"The victim was lying face down on the car when I arrived. Residents on the lower floors were outside on their balconies. One person stood over there on the sidewalk. None of the people I spoke to saw the victim fall, but they all heard it." The officer pulled out a small notebook. "Mr. Lum, the guy standing near the car when I arrived, was the first to call 911. He stated that he had just finished using the bathroom and was getting ready to climb back into bed when he heard a loud crash. He came out on his balcony, thinking there was a vehicle collision. That's when he saw the body on the car."

"Which apartment does Mr. Lum live in?" Bennie asked before he popped the last bite of his cruller into his mouth.

"That's his apartment on the second floor, right behind the car."

"And the victim's apartment? Sokolov asked."

"Straight up. The penthouse on the top floor."

Bennie walked around to the other side of the car and stood on the sidewalk. He looked up. "Jumping from there with a slight push outward would be enough to clear the sidewalk and hit the car. Men jump outwards from a building, whereas women tend to drop straight down."

"If that's the case, he did a perfect swan dive," Delgado said.

"Do you know if the victim was alone at the time?"

"It took a while before the building manager could get here and let me into the apartment. There's a chance someone might

11

have been with him and left before I could get up there. It looked like Mr. Tiller was having a small party...there were open liquor bottles and a dusting of what appeared to be a controlled substance on a glass coffee table. Probably cocaine. CSI is in the apartment now."

"Where's the manager?" Bennie asked.

"Her name is Peggy Meyer," Delgado said as he looked around. "She might have stepped back inside the building. Her office is directly inside and to the left. She's got long blonde hair."

"No doorman or night security?" Sokolov asked.

"They have a doorman, but he only works during the day. No security guard at night. No security cameras in the entire building."

"No cameras on any of the floors?" Bennie asked with surprise.

"According to the manager, it's an old building, and cameras were left out from the get-go. They tried to put them in later, but the residents voted it down, preferring their privacy. Have either of you been inside?"

Sokolov and Bennie both shook their heads.

"I've been inside three times. Tonight makes four. It's essentially the same building now as when it was first built thirty-five years ago. Nothing about it has changed. Many people in the building have lived here since it opened."

"Anything else to tell us before we head up?" Sokolov asked.

Delgado shook his head. "If something else comes up, I'll let you know."

The front door to the building was propped open, so Sokolov and Bennie headed straight inside. A woman with blonde hair was leaning against a wall and looking at her phone.

"Ms. Peggy Meyer?" Sokolov asked.

The woman looked up. "Yes, I'm her, and it's 'Mrs.' But you

can call me Peggy. You two must be the detectives I've been told to wait for."

"I'm Detective Sokolov, and this is Detective Bennie. I apologize for keeping you waiting."

"Please, I had a dead body outside until twenty minutes ago. There's no crawling back into bed after that."

"You live in the building?" Bennie asked before draining the last of his coffee and tossing the cup in a nearby trash can.

"My husband and I live across the bay in Tiburon. It's why it took a while for me to get here on such short notice."

"Nobody really plans for dead bodies," Bennie said with a sympathetic smile.

"Would you mind taking us up to Mr. Tiller's apartment?" Sokolov asked.

"Yes, of course." She led the way to the elevator. "A keycard is required to access the building, but once you're in, you don't need it to get to a particular floor. It's the only security feature this building has, aside from the daytime doorman."

"Has it always been like that?" Bennie asked.

She nodded. "That's part of the charm of the building. Nothing much has changed over the years."

"How many apartments are on the top floor?"

"There are only two penthouse suites. Errol—I mean, Mr. Tiller—owns one. Mr. Yang owns the other suite. He and his family spend most of their time in China. They visit for, like, a month, twice a year at the most. So Mr. Tiller pretty much has the top floor all to himself."

The elevator doors opened, and they stepped inside the car.

"Are either of you familiar with the building?" Peggy asked.

"We're not," Sokolov answered. "What can you tell us?"

"All of the units are owner occupied. Leasing out an apartment is not allowed. It prevents the place from becoming transient."

"Unless you're Mr. Yang," Bennie said with a smile.

"He's in the penthouse, so his residency doesn't really affect the others in the building."

The doors opened, and Peggy made a right, leading the way down the hall to Tiller's apartment. The front door had been propped open.

"Peggy, we'll need some time in here, but we'd like to continue our conversation when we're done," Sokolov said.

"Of course. I'll be downstairs in my office."

Sokolov and Bennie headed inside and saw a tech with CSI, examining the kitchen counter.

"Guillermo," Bennie called out. "I see you got lucky just like us."

Guillermo turned around to face them. "Good morning, detectives. Yeah, I don't know why I always get early-morning calls." He rested his hands on his hips. "At least this appears to be a case we can put together fairly quickly."

"You think it's definitely suicide?" Sokolov asked.

"All signs point to it, but I'll let you guys do your job. Come on, let me show you around."

Guillermo led the way past the large open kitchen area to the center of the apartment. To the left was a large living room area. To the right was the smaller sitting room. Both had balconies. Standing directly in the middle provided a view of the bay, if you looked right, or inland to Nob Hill, if you looked left.

"It seems Mr. Tiller liked to party," Guillermo said. "We have multiple open liquor bottles. The white dust on the glass coffee table is cocaine. I'm guessing there was more, but it was inhaled; we'll see what the toxicology report comes back with. He definitely had guests here recently. I can't say if it was last night, but it's your job to determine that."

"Were you able to pull prints?" Sokolov asked.

"I was. There were a lot. In addition to the prints, I bagged strands of long hair. One blonde and one brunette. I lifted a few strands of short brown hair off the floor in the master bedroom, most likely Tiller's. I also found short black hair. UV light shows bodily fluids on the bedsheets and the sofa in the living room. I didn't detect any blood droplets anywhere in the apartment. Once I get back to the lab, I'll run the prints and test for DNA. Other than that—I don't see any signs of a break-in or a struggle. If someone was with him when he went over, he probably knew the person."

Sokolov walked out to the balcony facing Nob Hill. "No sign of a struggle out here, either."

"The balcony railing is regulation height, but it is possible he got wasted and accidentally fell over. If that had happened, he would have dropped straight down and hit the sidewalk. He landed on a car several feet out, so I'm inclined to believe he pushed away from the balcony."

"Or was thrown," Bennie said.

"That is a possibility. Did you see the body before it was taken away?"

"No."

"Tiller looked to be about five feet ten inches with average proportions. Someone with Sokolov's height and mass, I think, could have easily tossed him over the railing. Someone smaller with a running head start also could have pushed with enough force to put him on the right trajectory to hit that car."

"No alcohol or glasses outside here," Bennie noted. "All the partying happened inside."

"Yeah, seems that way." Guillermo turned and headed back inside. "The master bedroom is this way."

Sokolov remained outside on the balcony for a moment, staring at the homes on Nob Hill, before catching up with the others.

Chapter Four

Jill

EVERY SATURDAY MORNING, from eight to two, there was a farmers' market at the Ferry Building. It had become a habit for me to meet my friend Helen Carr at a café there. We'd have breakfast and catch up before strolling around and doing some shopping. It had been two weeks since I'd last seen Helen. She'd been busy with her online business, a successful little candle shop that she'd built up over the last couple of years called No Bull Scent.

Helen wasn't originally from the Bay Area. She was a strong-minded, proudly independent woman from Queens, New York. Her father was Irish, and her mother was Puerto Rican. As Helen had recounted it, you had to be tough to grow up mixed in her neighborhood. And I loved that brash side of her. In fact, I admired it and often wished I could be more like her. In the meantime, I settled for being her friend.

When I arrived, Helen was already sitting inside the café and looking over the menu.

"Sorry I'm late," I said.

She waved off my apology as she yawned. "I just got here

myself, but I'm starved. I'm getting the ham and cheese omelet with fried potatoes. What about you?"

"I'm not hungry. I think I'll just have some yogurt."

"Suit yourself." She motioned for the server.

After we put in our order, Helen leaned in. "So, did you hear?"

"Is that what we're talking about first?"

"And why the hell not? Surely you don't want to hear about the gift show I was at all week."

"Did you see the body?" I asked.

"No, it was already gone by the time I walked out of the building, but the car he hit was being towed away. Apparently, he landed right on it. Practically flattened the roof. You should have seen the reporters from the news jockeying for position. It's a madhouse. I hope those news vans aren't there when I get home."

"They didn't mention on the news that he hit a car."

"Of course, they won't say that. I can only imagine the noise he made on impact."

"Thanks for that image and sound bite. So, did you hear it?"

"Not from my side. Plus, I'm a deep sleeper."

Helen lived on the fifth floor of the Residence and faced the bay. I'd been inside her apartment numerous times; it was a lovely two-bedroom and perfect for her.

"But the people on the second and third floor, where that car was parked? I guarantee that woke them up."

"I'm sure it did."

The image of the body passing through the telescope's field of view popped into my mind. I still hadn't told anyone what I'd seen, and I debated whether or not to even mention it to Helen. But I didn't want our entire morning to be consumed by Errol's death. I figured I'd let Helen get it out of her system, and then we'd move on to a conversation that wasn't about death or dying.

The server stopped by and dropped off our food. I thought that would distract Helen. It didn't.

"Did the news mention how Errol died?" Helen asked as she cut into the omelet. "I mean, I know *how* he died, but you know what I'm talking about."

"They didn't say a thing about that in the newscast I watched. They just kept saying it was tragic."

"'Tragic'? Why is everything so tragic nowadays? Thousands of people die every day. Why does Errol's death get the 'tragic' label? Anyway, I think he jumped."

"Suicide?"

"Sure."

"But why would he kill himself? I didn't know him that well, but he always seemed like a pretty happy guy whenever I'd see him at a charity function."

"You'd be surprised how well someone can hide their depression."

"Well, I guess he could have been depressed. Still, it's very shocking to think of that."

"What? You think it was accidental, like he got drunk and fell over the railing?" Helen shoved a large bite of omelet into her mouth.

I shrugged as I stirred my spoon around in my yogurt.

"It's possible. Of course, there's the other option." Helen leaned as she swallowed and softly said, "Murder."

"You think?"

Now it was Helen's turn to shrug, as she forked another bite into her mouth. "This is so good. Do you want to try?"

I shook my head. "You can't be serious about what you said?"

"I'm just saying. You said you didn't know Errol that well. So why not? But honestly, my money's on suicide." Helen yawned again.

"You keep yawning. Am I boring you?"

"I went to bed late last night, that's all."

"So how well did *you* know him?" I asked. "You've been living in that building for two years."

"Same as you. We'd say 'hi' when we passed in the lobby or have as much small talk as we could on a ride up to my floor. Actually, I never saw him with anyone in the building—you know, like hanging out or having an in-depth conversation. Seemed like a private person."

"You know, Mia did an internship for him this past summer."

"That's right. I forgot all about that. How did it go?"

"It went well, according to her. I do hope his sudden death doesn't taint it for her. I also hope it doesn't affect her college applications. She has her heart set on Stanford. It's so competitive, and I keep hearing how little things can make or break an application."

"I wouldn't worry about it. Errol was well known in San Francisco, but I think the farther you go outside the city, the less known he is. I wonder what will happen to his company now that he's gone? As far as I know, he wasn't married and didn't have any kids."

"Maybe he has other family. Or maybe his partners will take it over."

"Jill, you've been stirring that spoon around in your yogurt since the waiter put it in front of you. Either eat it or pass it over here."

I took a bite. "Last night was date night with Alan."

"How did that go? Did you guys bang?"

"Sheesh, Helen. Do you have to call it that?"

"Sorry, 'make love.'" She rolled her eyes at me.

"Alan had a last-minute client thing that ate up the entire

night. I finished two bottles of wine alone, waiting for him to hurry home."

"Where were the kids?"

"Mia was at a sleepover, and Ollie went camping with his friend, Grant. You know the Walkers, right? Kelly and Kent? They live in your building."

"Yeah, seventeenth floor. I know them. But very surface level. The husband seems nicer to me than the wife. She comes across as a little standoffish."

"Yeah, I can see that."

"Well, it's a shame about your sexless date night."

"Dateless date night," I corrected her. "I was really looking forward to spending quality time with Alan."

"Yeah, you two could have had 'quality time' all night long," Helen said, making exaggerated air quotes.

I giggled. "I would have liked that. It's been a while since we did anything close. Even normal sex seems impossible, between the kids, and Alan's work, and..."

"You need a vibrator. I'm buying you one—you'd like the one I have."

"I don't need a vibrator," I scoffed.

"Yes, you do. End of story. In the meantime, try shower sex in the mornings."

"Ooh, you should create a candle with that name: Shower Sex," I said, spreading my hands in the air to create an imaginary marquee.

"That's a good idea. I think I will."

Chapter Five

SFPD

SOKOLOV AND BENNIE left Errol's suite after an hour of poking around. They didn't see anything that made them believe foul play was involved. Their assessment was that Tiller accidentally fell over the balcony or jumped willingly.

"I think that guy might have been stuck in a rough patch and decided to end it," Bennie said as they stepped into the elevator. "He drank and snorted until he was ready. Even if people were partying with him, they probably left before he jumped."

Sokolov nodded. "Tiller went over the railing around two in the morning. The first call goes in to 911 a few minutes later. Officer Delgado arrives within six minutes. If someone was with Tiller, there's a chance they blended in with the crowd and slipped away."

"Or they live in the building."

The two detectives walked toward the building manager's office, and Sokolov knocked on the doorframe as he peeked inside. Peggy sat behind her desk, consumed with her phone.

"Did we catch you at a bad time?" Sokolov asked.

"No. Please come inside and take a seat. Can I offer you a cup of coffee?"

They both shook their heads as they sat.

"So, how did everything go? Did you find what you were looking for?" Peggy asked.

"What is it you think we were looking for?" Sokolov asked.

She shrugged. "Oh, I don't know. Police stuff, I guess."

"Mrs. Meyer, how well did you know Mr. Tiller?"

"About as well as I know any of the people living in the building. We're friendly in the common areas, and 'hi' and 'hellos' are exchanged. I'm the building manager, so it's my job to interact with people, but I wouldn't say we were friends."

"Do you know if Mr. Tiller was friendly with anyone in the building? People he might have hung out with or grabbed a bite with?"

"Not that I know of, but he was very generous. You know, every Thanksgiving, he would hand out whole turkeys to anyone in the building who wanted one. During the Christmas holiday, he always organized a toy drive for local charities and placed a present under the tree in the lobby for every child in the building. He was well liked by everyone in the building. I never had a single complaint about him. But every time I saw him, he was alone."

Peggy ran a hand through her long hair.

"Do you ever enter any of the apartments by yourself?" Sokolov asked.

"Occasionally, I might have a need, but with the owner's permission, of course. Usually, I try to meet with people in my office. I'll either call or send them a note to stop by on their way in or out."

Sokolov cleared his throat. "Did you enter Mr. Tiller's apartment this morning?"

"Briefly, when I let the police officer inside. And I only stood in the doorway. I was too afraid to go inside."

"And outside that instance, when was the last time you were in Mr. Tiller's apartment?"

Peggy drew a deep breath. "Whew, it's been a while. It might have been when he first moved in, years ago. I never had a reason to. I think, once, he stopped by to file a maintenance request."

"Who handles those requests?"

"That would be Ray Evans, the building superintendent. Ray has an office below us, on the basement level. Residents can either fill out a request form here, or they can call him direct if it's an emergency. Most people call him direct, because it's faster and easier."

"Does Mr. Evans work alone?"

"He has an assistant. His name is Darrel Knight."

Sokolov made a note of both names.

"Mrs. Meyer, how long have you been the building manager?"

"Almost fifteen years. Started off as an assistant to the previous building manager. When he retired, I was elevated to this position. No one replaced me in my old position. There's really no need for it."

"Who is in charge of staffing? You?"

"When I was an assistant to the building manager, the building's board of directors would make those decisions."

"And who are these board members?"

"Residents who lived in the building. But shortly after I took over, the residents voted to remove the board. If any big decisions are made, it comes down to a vote among all the residents. It's straightforward: I put a note in their mailboxes asking them to check a box. After, I tally up the results, and we have a decision. But most of the residents trust me to make most of the decisions around here."

"Was it your decision not to have security cameras on every floor and in the elevators?" Bennie asked.

"That was a suggestion to the residents a while ago. People here value their privacy, so they voted 'no.' We used to have a twenty-four-hour doorman. Now we just have someone who works the day shift: nine to five. He should be here by now. His name is Guy Sharp."

"Do you work the same hours?" Sokolov asked.

"I'm usually in by eight and out by five. Work-life balance is important to me, but occasionally I need to stick around a little later."

"You mentioned earlier that Mr. Tiller had the entire floor to himself for most of the year."

"That's correct."

"And none of the other people who live in the building have access to that floor?"

"They do, because a keycard isn't needed to access each floor. But people here respect each other's privacy."

Sokolov crinkled his brow. "But a keycard is needed to enter the building, right?"

"That's correct. You have to understand, detectives. This building was built a long time ago. People get used to things being a certain way and don't want to change."

"Who lives in the apartment below Mr. Tiller?"

"Well, technically, there are two apartments below him. One faces Nob Hill, and Barbara Ezra lives in that one. The other apartment is actually on the market. The current owners moved out about four months ago. They're asking a lot for the place, which is why it's still empty. But if you're interested in talking to Ms. Ezra, she's in apartment 3108."

Sokolov wrote the information down. "I think we'll swing by the superintendent's office first."

"Sure, just hit 'B' in the elevator."

————————

Sokolov and Bennie waited until the elevator doors closed before speaking.

"Thoughts?" Bennie asked.

"So far, Tiller seems like a nice guy. He was well liked in the building. Charitable. Why would he kill himself? Problem with an ex? Problems at the office?"

"Yeah, my thoughts as well. But Mrs. Meyer...she's got a lot of control in the building for a manager. She makes most of the decisions without a board of directors to answer to. She decides what goes to a vote. Not the way I'd like it if I lived here."

The elevator doors opened. Directly in front of them was a small office. The door was open, and a man was sitting behind a desk.

"Mr. Ray Evans?" Sokolov asked.

"That's me. I'm guessing you two are with the police. You're here to talk about what happened earlier?"

"That's correct. I'm Detective Sokolov, and this is my partner, Detective Bennie. Is now a good time?"

"As good a time as any. Take a load off." Evans gestured to a pair of folding chairs facing his desk.

Evans looked to be in his late fifties. He had a buzz cut, a squared-off jaw, and a stare that screamed "ex-military." Appeared fit for his age.

"Mr. Evans, could you tell us what time you arrived this morning?"

"Got down here as soon as I could after Peggy, Mrs. Meyer,

called. I live in San Bruno, so it's quite a bit away. It must have been close to four when I arrived."

"How well did you know Mr. Tiller?"

"Outside of his maintenance issues? Well enough to say 'hi' and ask how everything was in passing. Nice guy—tipped well during the holidays. Gave me a thousand bucks this past Christmas. But I always got the sense that he preferred to keep to himself. I think he's one of those people who are always surrounded by others asking for his time, so when he wasn't being hounded, he valued time alone. It's the opposite for me." Ray motioned around his office. "Not much happening down here."

"You have an assistant, right?" Sokolov double-checked his notes. "Darrel Knight?"

"Yup. He just had a kid, so he had some sort of doctor's check-up he needed to be at this morning. He'll be in a little later."

"Does he know what happened?"

"Yeah, I told him about Mr. Tiller. But even if I hadn't, it's all over the news."

"Did Tiller have a lot of maintenance issues?"

"Not that I can recall. But let me look it up. We log most of the maintenance calls."

"Why only most and not all?" Bennie asked.

"Sometimes it's so minor, like screwing in a light bulb that the owner is having difficulty reaching. We should log everything. That's what I'm trying to do with this system. When I first got here, nothing was kept track of. It's better now, but we still have a ways to go. Okay, here we go. Looks like the last request came about two months ago. He had a leaky faucet."

"Mr. Evans, do you know if Mr. Tiller had problems with any of the other residents?" Sokolov asked.

"Not that I can recall, but he did enjoy his alcohol. One

night, I was leaving late and bumped into him in the lobby. He had two crates of wine that he needed help carrying. So I helped him get the bottles up to his apartment. Did you know the guy has a temperature-controlled wine storage unit in his apartment? It's impressive."

Sokolov and Bennie spent a few more minutes questioning Mr. Evans. He mainly had the same things to say as Mrs. Meyer, so they thanked him for his time and left.

Sokolov and Bennie stepped out of the elevator on the thirty-first floor and made their way to apartment 3108. They knocked. A moment later, the door cracked open, and a tiny, elderly woman peered up at them through a pair of tortoise-shell-framed glasses.

"What do you want?" she asked with a slight frown as she looked them over.

"Ms. Barbara Ezra?" Sokolov held up his identification. "I'm Detective Sokolov, and this is Detective Bennie. Do you have a moment to answer a few questions?"

Ms. Ezra pulled the door back and stepped out of the way. "I was knitting, but I suppose I could use a break. I'm assuming you're here to talk about what happened this morning." She shuffled into the living room.

"That's right."

"Can I fix you something to drink? Tea?"

"No, thank you."

"Have a seat." She motioned to the sofa before sitting in an armchair, her feet barely touching the carpeted floor. "I'll start by saying I didn't know Errol Tiller very well. I'd see him every now and then in the lobby, but that was it. I heard him more than I saw him."

"'Heard'? Could you expand on that?"

"Moaning. I'd hear it occasionally when I was sitting on my balcony. Sometimes it sounded like soft crying. I couldn't tell sometimes."

"Was he alone?"

"I suppose, unless he was moaning and someone else was crying."

"But you're sure the moaning was him—a man's voice."

"Sometimes it sounded like a man, and sometimes it didn't. It was pitched higher."

"So maybe a woman?"

"Maybe. If you're wondering if the noises were sexual, they could have been. But I know what normal sex sounds like, and I don't think that was normal. And if you find out, I don't want to know. Whenever I'd hear it, I'd come back inside."

"So these noises, did they occur often?"

"Maybe once a week. I don't go out much at my age, so I'm always around. I have most things delivered to me."

"You live alone, then?"

"Yes. My children are all grown and live in Chicago, where I'm originally from. When my husband passed, I sold the house and moved out here. My children thought I was nuts, but I've always loved this city since I first visited as a young woman."

Sokolov leaned forward. "Ms. Ezra, did it sound like Mr. Tiller had visitors often?"

"I can't say for sure, but it would be strange if he was alone making those noises. I'd also hear thumping, almost as if he were stomping on the floor or jumping. But that was just on occasion. I didn't report him to building manager for that."

"Did you report the moaning?"

"I did, but nothing came of it."

"Did you hear any loud music or conversation?"

"No, nothing like that."

"Did you hear any strange noises last night?"

"No. And if you're wondering if I heard him jump off his balcony, I didn't."

"What makes you think he jumped?"

"I just assumed that's what happened. He didn't?"

"That's what we're trying to determine."

"I guess he could have fallen by accident."

Barbara leaned back, turning her head toward her own balcony as she stared into the distance.

"Do you mind if we take a closer look at your balcony?" Sokolov stood.

Barbara nodded absentmindedly. "The door should be open. I'll wait here, if it's all right with you."

"Nice view," Bennie said as they looked out at Nob Hill.

Sokolov poked his head out over the railing and looked up. "His balcony is right there. She could easily hear him if he was outside, but why would he be moaning outside?"

"He was probably with some woman on the balcony, or he likes to leave the balcony door open."

They headed back inside.

"Did it help any?" Barbara asked.

"Everything helps," Sokolov said. "We appreciate you taking the time to speak with us."

"You're welcome." She pushed herself up off the chair and smoothed out her blouse. "There is something else that comes to mind. Do you know what happened to the dog?"

"What dog?"

Chapter Six

Jill

I PARTED ways with Helen at noon and headed home. Usually, our Saturday brunch outings lasted well into the afternoon, but Helen had candle issues she had to deal with. It was fine with me; I was still a bit hungover from the previous night. I parked in my driveway and headed inside. Mia was already home. I could hear her talking to someone in the kitchen.

"Hi, Mom," she said.

She was on a video call with a friend.

"How was your sleepover?" I asked as I bent down to kiss her head.

"It was great."

I recognized her friend on the call. "Hi, Michele."

"Hi, Mrs. Pittman."

"Mia, is your father home?"

"You just missed him. He went to the store to buy ground beef for hamburgers tonight."

I placed a bag of fresh fruits and vegetables on the countertop. "Mia, will you do me a favor and put those away? Thank you."

I headed upstairs to my bedroom. Ever since Helen and I had started talking about Errol's death, I couldn't wait to get home and take another peek into his apartment with the telescope. It still ate away at me that I might have seen Errol fall. I realized it was a quick blip...and I had been drinking, and my memory of that split second was fuzzy, but I think I would know if I saw the falling body. I was ninety percent sure that's what I saw.

But why did it matter? Was I the only one in this city of thousands who saw Errol fall? We weren't the only people who lived on Nob Hill. Surely someone else had been up at that hour, looking toward the bay.

But were they looking through a telescope at the building?

That didn't matter. I couldn't have been the only one.

Are you sure?

I certainly leaned that way.

I brought one of Alan's telescopes onto our balcony and looked through the eyepiece. It took a bit of maneuvering before I was able to lock on to Errol's apartment.

Huh, there are two men in the apartment. They're definitely with the police department, probably detectives.

The tall one rested his hands on his waist while he looked around. The other got down on his knees and looked under the sofa.

The tall one made his way out to the balcony. He had a concentrated look on his face, like he was working through a problem. Suddenly, his eyes locked on me, and I drew a sharp breath.

Calm down, Jill. He's not actually looking at you. He's only looking in your direction.

I did wonder what it was that troubled him. I sort of knew Errol, so I had an interest. The news continued to report that suicide was the most likely cause of Errol's death. Was this man questioning that? Did he believe it was an accident? Or worse, that someone pushed Errol?

Could murder really be an option here? Errol was wealthy; maybe someone wanted his money. But he was so charitable. He was always giving back to the community. I don't think I ever heard the word "no" come out of his mouth. He barely knew me, and still he had arranged for Mia to have an internship at his company in an instant. I really found it hard to believe he would have enemies. Plus he was named San Francisco's most eligible bachelor. You don't get that title by being a schmuck, right?

The suited man on Errol's balcony looked over the railing for a moment, probably imagining the fall. He bent at the knee, and it looked like he was putting his eye up to something. I adjusted the telescope's focus and sharpened my view a tad bit more. That was when I realized Errol also owned a telescope, and the man was looking through it. Suddenly he raised his head away from the telescope and squinted in my direction.

Crap!

I pulled the telescope back into the bedroom and quickly closed the sheer drapes.

Oh, my God. Did he see me looking at him? No, it can't be... But it looked like he did. Crap! Crap!

I stuck the tip of the telescope through a narrow opening in the drapes and took another look. The man had already headed back inside the apartment.

You're overthinking this stuff. It's a big hill, Jill. What are the odds of him zeroing in on you?

Chapter Seven

Alan Pittman

I HADN'T SPOKEN to my wife since Friday morning when I left for work. I remembered kissing her on the lips and telling her I had a naughty evening planned for her. And then, when I got to the office, a big pile of crap was dumped onto my parade. It had been a long time since I'd been able to give Jill the best of Alan, if you catch my drift. Just thinking about it made me rise to the occasion.

Jill's car was parked in the driveway when I got home. I figured it would be easy to persuade Mia to hang out with her friends so Jill and I could have some time alone to make up for last night.

I slammed the front door shut behind me and headed toward the kitchen. Mia was sitting at the kitchen island, chatting on her phone and drinking a delivered Starbucks drink.

"Hey, kiddo. Where's my coffee?" I asked.

"Hi, Dad. It's in the fridge."

I opened the fridge and spotted the Starbucks version of the spritzy Americano: Orangina and two espresso shots. I was thirsty and needed a quick pick-me-up. I took the cup, replaced it with the ground beef I'd bought, and slammed the drink in one take.

"Whoa, Dad. Take it easy," Mia said.

"Is your mother upstairs?" I asked as I walked away, not waiting for an answer.

I hurried to the third floor and tiptoed the rest of the way to our bedroom. I wanted to surprise her.

When I reached the doorway, I poked my head inside. Jill was standing near the entrance to the balcony and peeking through the curtains. I took a moment to admire my wife. I'd always loved the way her chestnut hair draped across her back. And of course, there was her butt. I never got tired of looking at that. In fact, I loved watching my wife. She was as beautiful now as the first day I had laid eyes on her.

Step by step, I closed the distance between us. I could smell her perfume, Dior. Jill was shorter than me. The top of her head came right up to my Adam's apple. I reached out and slipped my arms around her waist, frightening her in the process. The top of her head slammed into my chin.

"Sheesh, Jill. You made me bite my tongue."

"What are you doing sneaking up on me like that?"

"I'm a lion hunting my prey."

She peeked out through the drapes again.

"What are you looking at?" I asked. This time, wrapping my arms around her didn't trigger the same reaction.

"Did you hear about Errol Tiller?" she asked.

"Yeah, terrible thing. Can you imagine leaping off of a building to your death? I shudder to think what his body must have looked like after."

"No need to paint the picture, Alan."

"Sorry. Are you upset? I didn't think you knew Errol all that well."

"I'm sad. I knew him from my charity work. Plus, he gave Mia that internship. It'll help with her college applications."

"That's true. Has the news reported anything new?" I asked, gripping Jill a little tighter.

"Not that I'm aware, but they keep alluding to suicide."

"That seems like the most likely explanation. It's not like Errol was a hated guy."

Jill turned and faced me. "Do you think it's possible it wasn't suicide or an accident?"

"What do you mean?"

"You know, like someone pushed him."

"I guess it's possible," I said as I nuzzled Jill's neck before kissing it. "But it's the police's job to determine that."

"Alan..."

"What?" I asked as I started running my hands over Jill's butt.

"Mia's home."

I pulled away from her neck and looked into her eyes. "Yeah, I know, but she's glued to that phone. And when, if ever, does she come up to our floor?"

"Hmm..."

I went back to nibbling Jill's neck. "I feel bad about last night. I want to make it up to you."

"And your plan is a quickie?"

"For now, yeah. Maybe Mia can go to another sleepover tonight, and we can have the place to ourselves. Remember the days before we had kids? When we would spend the entire day naked, only taking a break so I could pay the pizza delivery guy? We could do that tonight. What do you say?"

Jill's muscles relaxed as she snuggled in closer. "I like the sound of that."

I picked her up, walked over to the bedroom door, and kicked it closed before taking her to our bed.

"Wait, Alan, before we start—I have something to tell you."

"Unless it's about what you want me to do to you in the next ten minutes, I don't want to hear it."

"But it's bugging me, and if I don't get it out, it's all I'll think about."

I rolled off Jill and onto my side to face her. "Okay, what's on your mind?"

"I think I saw Errol fall last night."

I sat up. "What? How?"

"Well, I was drinking a glass of wine last night..."

"More like two bottles." I laughed.

Jill hit me playfully.

"Shut up and listen. I was sitting out on the balcony and decided to take a peek through your telescope. I wasn't looking at anything in particular, but I had the telescope pointed at the building, and that's when I saw it...or I think I saw it. It was a quick blip, but it looked like a body falling. I was so shocked that I pulled away and looked at the building with my naked eye."

"And?"

"Well, I didn't see anything. Plus, I was blinking, thinking I must have had something in my eye."

"So you had a piece of dust in your eye."

"But I've been thinking about this all day. I don't think that was it. I think I saw Errol fall."

I rolled over onto my back. "Hmm."

"What do you think we should do? Should we report this to the police?"

"What? That you think you saw Errol fall?" I shook my head. "Look, they'll start asking questions, like 'Why were you up so late?' 'Why were you watching his apartment through a telescope?'"

"But I wasn't."

"I know that, but they don't. That's what they'll assume.

And then they'll start wondering if you had anything to do with it. I know I'm making big leaps, but it's so random that you saw this. And you're not even one hundred percent sure." I turned back to Jill. "You're not, right?"

"I'm not."

"There you go. Plus, do you want to tell the police that you polished off two bottles of wine all by yourself?"

"It was a bottle and a half."

"I found two empty bottles when I got home."

"By the way, what time did you come home?"

"I'm not sure. Late, and you were already passed out."

"Did you drink a lot?"

"Not really, but my clients did. One even took a tumble toward the end of the night. I had to help them back to their hotel, where they insisted on a few more nightcaps. They were both wasted when I left, but they had a good time. Look, forget about this falling business. It doesn't matter—"

"But what if—"

I pressed my finger against Jill's lips. "If you had looked through the telescope a split second later, we wouldn't even be having this conversation. And what does telling the police this really add to their investigation?"

"Probably nothing."

I grabbed hold of Jill and brought her into me. "So let's forget about it for now. All you saw was Errol falling. You don't know how or why he fell, just that he fell." I started kissing Jill on the neck. "We have more pressing matters to deal with."

Chapter Eight

SFPD

SOKOLOV AND BENNIE were on their way back down to the lobby after revisiting Tiller's apartment.

"If he did have a dog, he either got rid of it a while ago, or he was fostering it," Bennie said during the elevator ride.

"That could be it. We keep hearing about his involvement in charities; maybe he was working with a rescue," Sokolov said. "Still, if he did foster dogs, where are the chew toys and the water bowl? There wasn't even a leash."

"I'm texting the guys in the lab to check if any of the hairs they collected were canine."

"Maybe whoever he was drinking and snorting with took the dog."

"So far, all we got is that Tiller was nice and generous," Bennie said. "No known enemies. Also, what about family? No one has come by to ask about him."

"Maybe he ain't got any. It'll be good to get his colleagues' takes on him." Sokolov glanced at his watch. "It's Saturday. I wonder if anyone is even at the office."

"We could stop by on the way back to the station, but it's also no biggie to wait until Monday. This isn't a hot case."

They stepped out of the elevator and ran into a man who seemed in a hurry.

"Sorry, my bad," the man said. "Hey, wait—you guys with SFPD?"

"Yeah," Sokolov answered.

"I've been looking for you. My boss said you might have some questions for me. I'm Darrel Knight, the super's assistant."

"We appreciate you taking the time to find us. I'm Detective Sokolov, and this is Detective Bennie. Let's step off to the side over there."

"What can you tell us about your relationship with Mr. Tiller?"

"It was strictly professional. The only time we interacted was if he had a maintenance issue. Besides that, he'd always say 'hi' to me when he saw me around. He congratulated me when my wife gave birth to my son."

"Could you tell us the last time you had to address a maintenance issue for Mr. Tiller?"

"I guess it was last month. He had a dripping faucet. A simple fix that took five minutes, tops."

"Are you sure it was last month?"

"Uh, yeah. Why?"

"We spoke to you supervisor earlier and he looked up the last request. It was two months ago."

"You know all these requests start to look the same. He's probably right."

"Which faucet was it?"

"It was the kitchen faucet. Why?"

"Did you notice a dog when you were in there?"

"Yeah, it's a little guy. Heavy breather."

"And this was a month ago?"

"Yeah... Did something happen to the dog?"

"We're not sure. It's not there now."

"Maybe he gave it up for adoption. Mr. Tiller seemed like a busy man, always coming and going."

"We appreciate your time, Mr. Knight." Sokolov handed him a business card. "If you remember something else we should know, that's my direct number on the card."

"That's it?"

"That's it."

———

Sokolov and Bennie arrived at Tiller & Associates, having decided to give the offices a visit on the off chance someone would be working on a Saturday. The place was located in the SoMa district, an area known for its many warehouses that were converted into housing and offices. Tiller's company was head-quartered in one such warehouse.

"If the name is any indication, then he's got business part-ners," Sokolov said.

The front door was made of steel, with a narrow section of glass off to the left that allowed them to see inside.

"The lights are off. We might be out of luck," Bennie said as he peered through the glass. "Oh, wait. I think I see someone." Bennie knocked on the glass. "He sees us. He's coming."

A man dressed in a white polo and khakis opened the door. "May I help you?"

Sokolov held up his ID and introduced himself and Bennie. "Do you mind if we come inside and ask you a few questions about Mr. Tiller?"

"No, not at all. You actually came at the right time. My name is Phillip Benson. I'm one of the managing partners at Tiller & Associates. In fact, all of the managing partners are here today because of what happened to Errol. We're all in a state of shock. We never in a million years could have imagined this happening." Benson paused, shaking his head, then waved the detectives through the door. "Come back this way. We're in the conference room."

Benson led the way down a long hallway. Three other people were sitting around a large oak table. Coffee mugs, left-over takeout, and numerous papers were scattered across it.

"Guys, I'd like you to meet Detectives Sokolov and Bennie. They've stopped by to ask a few questions about Errol."

The partners mumbled "hello."

"This is Ginnie Franklin," Benson said. "She's head of our media department. The guy that looks like he hasn't shaved in ten years is Rook Carter, our creative director. And this snap-pily dressed fella is Simon Friedman. He's head of account services. Did you want to question us individually or together? How does this work?"

"You're doing a fine job so far. Let's see how it goes," Sokolov said. Then, turning to address the group, he continued, "I'm assuming you all knew Mr. Tiller fairly well. Were any of you aware of any personal or professional problems Mr. Tiller might have had?"

Benson gave everyone around the table a look before turning back to Sokolov. "I'll cut to the chase. Our relationship with Errol had deteriorated over the last year. He was no longer the same person we'd all grown to love."

"Why is that?"

"We've discussed this over the hill and back, but we can't figure it out. He just started acting differently—less responsible, becoming forgetful, stumbling over his words. It wasn't like Errol. He was always quick on his feet, focused, and charming. Regarding his work ethic, he was a first-one-in-the-office, last-one-out type of guy. He could be dead tired, but he'd sit down and help a person out if needed."

"But that stopped," Sokolov prodded.

"Yes. We think it started with the alcohol. He started drinking more at company functions and client outings. In fact, he set up a wet bar in his office so he could day drink like we were still the ad men of the sixties. And then we started losing clients. One by one, they left... We had a responsibility to this company. We couldn't stand by and watch the place burn down." Benson drew a deep breath and let it out slowly. "Three months ago, we—the people in this room—decided to approach Errol about his behavior. We told him we could no longer allow him to run this place into the ground. We wanted him to check into a rehabilitation center for drugs and alcohol. We were fully willing to support him and do whatever it took to help him get better. But he outright refused. It went downhill quickly from there. We had no choice but to tell him we were buying him out of his company. And that was that."

"How did he take the news?" Bennie asked.

"Not well. He told us all to eff off and walked out of the building. You have to believe that we all loved Errol. We were doing everything we could to help him, but nothing we tried worked. The company was and still is experiencing dire financial constraints. A couple of days ago, he sent us all an email agreeing to work on an exit plan that was suitable for everyone. And then we heard the news this morning."

"In the last week, did any of you contact Mr. Tiller outside the office?" Sokolov asked.

Everyone in the room shook their head.

"Did Mr. Tiller have administrative support?" Bennie asked.

"Yes, Alice has been by his side since he started this place. She's actually here today helping us pull paperwork together."

"Where is she? We'd like to speak with her."

Benson pointed to the doorway. "Go left, and it's the large

office at the end of the hall. That's Errol's office. You'll find Alice in there."

On the way to Tiller's office, Bennie checked his messages on his phone. "The lab confirmed that one of the hairs they retrieved was canine."

"I guess Ms. Ezra wasn't kidding about a dog being there."

The two stopped in the doorway of the office. A bunch of filing boxes were spread across the floor, and a woman wearing glasses was on her knees looking through them. Sokolov cleared his throat and made the usual introductions.

Alice stood and smoothed her blouse. "It's a terrible time. I can't believe he's gone."

"Mr. Benson mentioned that you were with Mr. Tiller from the beginning."

"That's correct. He and I were in a small office when we first started. You know, at its height, this place was thriving. Two hundred people worked here, and rarely did they leave unless it was for a better opportunity. People genuinely enjoyed working for Errol. But now we've lost a bunch of business and have fewer than forty people after all the layoffs. Such a shame." Alice looked off to the side and appeared to wipe away a tear. "He changed."

"How so?"

"Errol was a friend to everyone. He could make anyone around him feel instantly comfortable, as if you had known him for years. But there was a side of Errol that people didn't know about. He was troubled. I don't know what these demons were—and trust me, I tried talking to him about it, but he wouldn't have it. He'd smile and tell me everything was fine. I must have gotten so used to it over the years that it became who he was to me."

"Was he bipolar?" Sokolov asked.

"Probably, but his mood swings wouldn't happen often, nor

would they last very long. It was like he was aware of this side of himself, and as soon as it appeared, he'd work hard to bury it quickly. I urged him to go to therapy, but he always told me I was overthinking things. Over the last three months, his mood swings happened more frequently. I knew the partners were trying to push Errol out of his company. I won't pass judgment on whether that was right or wrong, but after they told him that, he went downhill quick. I'd walk in here some mornings and he'd be lost in thought, so much I'd have to shake him to get his attention. At times, he had trouble making simple decisions. It wasn't like him."

"What do you know about his drinking?" Sokolov asked.

"It had gotten much worse. Some days he'd be drunk by noon."

"Do you know if Mr. Tiller had a drug problem?"

"If he did, I never saw it. But I wouldn't be surprised. He'd be tired one minute and then full of energy the next. I'm no drug expert, but that is a sign."

"What about his personal life? Was he dating anyone? Did he have a family?"

"Both of his parents passed years ago, and Errol was an only child. He never did marry, but he dated a lot when I first came to work for him. Nothing ever got serious. Lately, I saw less and less of it. I used to make reservations for him at various restaurants in the city. That wasn't happening as much, especially in the past six months. For a long time, this place was his family... his life. He loved spending time here. Of course, there was his dog, Mr. Tiller. He loved that pug. On occasion, he even brought him into the office."

"He named his dog after himself?" Sokolov asked.

"I know. It's a bit corny."

"When was the last time you saw the dog?"

"It's been a while, a month or so at least. What will happen to Mr. Tiller? The dog?"

"We have no idea where the dog is. It wasn't there when we got to his apartment. Was it his dog, or was he watching it for someone?"

"Oh, well, that's a good question. I just assumed it was his. He only got it about six months ago. It could have belonged to another person, but why would he call it Mr. Tiller if it was someone else's dog?"

"Did Mr. Tiller receive any unusual calls recently?"

"I wouldn't say it was unusual, but I would label these calls annoying. They weren't business related. They were personal. Errol never took the calls, but this person called daily for the last couple of weeks. It was the same with every call. 'Yeah, can I speak to Errol? It's important,'" Alice mimicked.

"Do you have a number for this person?" Sokolov asked.

"Give me a minute to find it."

Alice grabbed a pen, wrote the number down on a piece of paper, and then handed it to Sokolov.

"He was very persistent, even though it was clear Errol was avoiding his calls," Alice said.

"Did he leave a name?"

"He just said to call Darrel."

"We appreciate your time," Sokolov said.

On the way out of the building, Bennie started shaking his head. "Just when it was looking like a slam dunk suicide."

Sokolov got out his cell and dialed the number Alice had given them. He switched over to speakerphone so Bennie could hear.

"Hi, you've reached the voicemail for Darrel Knight. Leave a message, and I'll get back to you soon."

"Looks like Mr. Knight lied to us," Sokolov said as he disconnected the call.

Chapter Nine

Helen Carr

THE NEWS VANS were gone when I returned to my apartment building. On the way in, I stopped to talk to Guy, our doorman.

"Welcome back, Ms. Carr," he said as he held the door open.

I looked around the lobby quickly. We were alone. "Hi, Guy, how is everything here?"

"You asking in the general sense, or is this regarding what happened to Mr. Tiller?"

"The second one."

"The cops are gone, but they questioned the staff."

"What did they ask you?"

"They wanted to know what kind of relationship I had with him and if I noticed anybody unusual visiting him."

"Was there? Anybody unusual, I mean."

"Not during the day when I'm here. Can't speak for what happens at night. My conversation lasted no more than a few minutes. It seemed like they were just going through the motions."

"Did they hint at what they thought had happened?"

"Nah, but Ms. Ezra told me they think it was suicide. No surprise there. I don't think anyone believes he fell by accident."

"How does she know what the police are thinking? Did they question her?"

"They did. But she told me after her conversation with them that they went back up to Mr. Tiller's apartment. She overheard the police talking on his balcony. You know Ms. Ezra, she's nosy."

"I see. Well, I'm glad the media circus from this morning is gone. I'm hoping things can get back to normal. Thanks, Guy."

"No problem, Ms. Carr. Enjoy the rest of your Saturday."

I was friendly with Barbara. We'd converse from time to time in the hallway and elevator, so I felt I knew her well enough to visit. I got off the elevator on her floor, headed to her apartment, and knocked. I waved when I saw her look through the peephole.

"Helen, what a pleasant surprise," she said when she opened the door. "Please, come inside."

"I'm sorry to come knocking unannounced."

"Don't be silly. Can I offer you a cup of tea?"

"Sure, that would be nice."

I took a seat in an armchair and waited for Barbara. About five minutes later, she reappeared from the kitchen with a tray holding two cups and a teapot. She placed it on the coffee table and poured tea into each mug.

"There's sugar in the bowl and cream in the creamer."

"Thank you." I added two sugars and a quick pour of cream.

"Can you believe it?" Barbara said before taking a sip.

"I'm still finding it hard to accept. Errol was the last person I would ever have expected to...well, it's not official yet."

"You mean 'jump'?"

I nodded.

"Well, you didn't hear this from me, but the police also think Errol jumped."

"How do you know?"

"They asked me questions this morning. I suppose it's because I live right below him."

"And they told you it was suicide?"

"No, not in those exact words, but I got the feeling that's what they were thinking. Then they decided to go back to Errol's apartment." A smile appeared on Barbara's face. "So I decided to enjoy the view on my balcony. That's when I heard them. They said the word 'suicide.' They're doing due diligence before they go on the record."

"You're probably right. They have that responsibility."

I'd been inside Barbara's apartment a couple of times. Nothing about the place had changed, except there was a familiar smell that I didn't associate with Barbara. I sniffed.

"Is that Shalimar I smell?"

"Oh God, yes. Peggy was here earlier. I swear she drowns herself in that perfume. It gives me a headache."

"That's the truth. You can always tell when Peggy's been around. Why was she here?"

"She wanted to know what the police had asked me."

"Really? I mean, I'm here for the gossip. But Peggy, she's the building manager. She shouldn't be gossiping, right?"

"I totally agree. But I guess she also has a responsibility. The police also questioned her."

"Do you know what they asked her?"

Barbara shook her head. "I didn't inquire. I didn't want to extend the conversation longer than needed."

I smirked knowingly—Peggy could be a talker.

"I just told her what questions the police asked me. They were normal ones, like 'How well did I know Errol?' 'When was the last time I saw him?' 'Was I aware of any problems he was having?' I did tell them about the strange noises."

"What noises?" I asked.

"Sometimes, I would hear moaning, or what sounded like crying. Once they realized I could hear what went on in his apartment, they asked about that night and if I heard anything strange or if I heard other people in his apartment. I didn't."

"I guess they'd want to know if he was alone. Crying—it's such a strange thing to hear coming from Errol. I never would have suspected. Maybe he knew what was coming and was mentally preparing himself...the reason for the crying noises," I said before taking a sip of my tea.

Barbara nodded her head in agreement. "If that's the case, he's been planning this for a while. I noticed the noises about three or four months ago."

Barbara glanced at the cuckoo clock on the wall.

"I hate to do this, but it's time for my afternoon nap. I'm afraid I'll pass out in the middle of our conversation if I don't lie down."

"Yes, of course. I've already taken up too much of your time. We can talk later," I said.

"I'd like that."

I hurried back down to my apartment. Once back inside, I immediately deleted the text messages between Errol and me. I also deleted my call history and the emails I sent to him and received. I knew damn well deleting that stuff on my end didn't mean it was gone. Communication between us could still be found on his devices. But I did it anyway.

Calm down, Helen. Don't read into it. The police are in the same camp as everyone else: Errol committed suicide.

I ignored my thoughts and signed into my PayPal account to delete the log of money transfers from Errol, but it wasn't allowed.

Shit! I knew I should have made these transactions cash only.

I couldn't believe the situation I was suddenly in. Just when I had finally steered my life in the right direction, this had to happen. I kept telling myself they knew nothing, but I wasn't very convincing.

They have to suspect foul play to dig around in Errol's financial affairs. They're thinking it's suicide. Barbara just confirmed it a few minutes ago. But what if they're not? What if Barbara heard wrong?

Chapter Ten

Jill

AFTER MY QUICK romp with Alan, I was feeling good and decided to get a start on the laundry. I stripped all the linens off our bed and then did the same in Mia's bedroom. I headed to Ollie's bedroom and started to undo his sheets from his bed when I heard a familiar noise: the click of a camera shutter.

I looked over at Ollie's camera. He had it mounted on a tripod with his long lens attached. I didn't know the exact name of the lens, but I knew that was what he used to shoot stuff in the distance. For a second, I thought I'd imagined it. Then I remembered I'd heard that sound the night before, when I switched off his desk lamp. I had thought the wine was making me hear things. Surely, the camera wasn't taking photos by itself. I didn't believe in ghosts, so that possibility didn't cross my mind. I continued to strip Ollie's bed when I heard the shutter go off again.

Now, I know I didn't imagine it this time.

I walked over to the camera. The LCD display on the back was dark, and it didn't look like the camera was turned on. The lens was pointed out his window, which wasn't strange to me; he could have been taking photos of birds, the city skyline, or the bay. I bent down so I could peer through the viewfinder.

The camera was pointed right at the Residence. Not at Errol's window, thank goodness, but directly at *someone's* apartment. The drapes on the balcony doors were drawn open, but no one was home. The lights were off. I didn't know who lived there, either. Helen was on the fifth floor, but faced the bay. I knew the building had thirty-two floors. So I counted down from the top floor. This apartment was on the fourteenth floor.

What on Earth is Ollie doing?

The shutter went off, and the LCD display lit up briefly. The camera had just taken a photograph of that apartment.

How does the camera take pictures automatically? More importantly, is Ollie spying on the person who lives there?

I tried my hardest not to assume the worst. But what was I supposed to think about a camera in my son's room that automatically took photos every few minutes of an apartment? *Oh, my God, is my son a Peeping Tom?*

Chapter Eleven

Jill – Fall of 1998, UCSB

I WAS ONLY three weeks into my first semester at the University of California at Santa Barbara and having a blast. Who knew college could be so fun? Certainly not me— I had lived a pretty sheltered life growing up. I was never outgoing and didn't rank anywhere near the most popular kid at school or in my neighborhood. Shy, nerdy, and awkward best described me. But I knew that people were allowed to reinvent themselves when they went off to college. And that was precisely what I intended to do.

UCSB was my number one choice when I applied to colleges, so when I got accepted, I was overjoyed. My parents were happy that I was going on to higher education and were willing to fund my four years there, so long as my GPA didn't drop below a 3.0. Of course, I hadn't quite realized UCSB was such a party school. I knew it had a reputation, but nothing could have prepared me for the substantial amount of free alcohol at my disposal.

My roommate, Sara, was from Los Angeles and was an expert at navigating the social scene on campus. Her older sister had graduated from UCSB the previous semester, and when

Sara was a senior in high school, she would drive up to Santa Barbara to party with her big sister. She may have been a freshman, but no one treated her that way. She was already a seasoned vet.

"Stick with me, Jill, and you'll get into all the popular parties and meet the right people," she told me.

I trusted Sara to lead me down the right path. My social skills were on life support, and I needed someone to help me breathe life back into them. Sara was that beacon of hope.

Sara took me by the hand from day one and helped me navigate the social scene. I'd met so many people within that first week, all because of Sara.

And the boys? She seemed to know every hunk on campus. Not only that, she introduced me to them. Sara told me she didn't believe in fighting over a guy and that there were plenty to go around. Did I enjoy the attention? Of course, I did. I felt like the most beautiful girl on campus. I was talking to so many boys I couldn't keep their names straight. Sara and I referred to them by nicknames. There was Surfer Boy and Mr. Blue Eyes, the Greek God and the New Yorker.

Sara had gotten us invited to a party at the most popular sorority on campus: Delta Gamma, or DG, as it was nicknamed. She told me all the cool kids would be there, and it was the place to be seen. The party was being held at the sorority house, a large, two-story building off campus. It was a beach theme, and everyone drank the jungle juice. It tasted delicious, but I learned early on that those fruity drinks were the ones that would knock you on your butt if you weren't careful.

Sara and I danced all night and drank a fair amount, but separated toward the end of the night. I had been talking to a boy when I realized I was suddenly tired. He kept telling me he would take me home and not to worry. But bringing a boy back to my room or going to his room was something I hadn't done yet. And to be honest, I was shy and a little scared.

My feet were starting to hurt, and I was ready to leave. When I found Sara, she was locking lips with a man who looked like he could be a bodybuilder.

"Sara," I said as I tapped her shoulder.

She broke away from him. "Jillllllllllllllll!" She slurred my name. "Are you having fun?"

"I am, but I'm tired. I think I'll head back to the dorm."

"Are you sure?"

"Yes. Will you be okay?"

"I'll be fine." She threw an arm around my neck and pulled me in so she could whisper into my ear. "Don't wait up," she shouted.

Our dorm was a fifteen-minute walk away. I wasn't worried about walking alone at night; there were always people out and about. Our room was on the first floor of the three-story building, at the end of the hall. We faced a wooded area. I liked it because it was quiet. Had our room been on the other end of the hall, there would have been a lot of foot traffic from the sidewalk directly out front.

The room was always stuffy, so the first thing I did whenever I got back was pull the drapes and open the windows to let fresh air inside. I fought my way out of my jeans and swapped my crop top for a comfy T-shirt.

Ah, so much better.

I plopped down at my desk, where my makeup bag and mirror were and used a wet wipe to clean my face. I was buzzed, but not enough to fall asleep with my makeup on. That was a surefire way to break out the next day.

Sara called asking if I had made it back to the dorm okay. She always did that. She also said she was definitely spending the night with the guy from the party, whom we dubbed "the

Bodybuilder." I'd seen him around campus; this wasn't the first time Sara had hooked up with him, so I wasn't too worried.

After cleaning my face, I stood in front of the full-length mirror that was affixed to the back of our door. I was a little concerned about gaining the infamous freshman fifteen. Alcohol would be the culprit. So far, I hadn't noticed any weight gain. I lifted my shirt up to just below my breasts to look at my stomach, hips, thighs, and butt.

After a few minutes of carefully eyeing every inch of my lower half, I concluded I was okay. We had a small fridge in the room that sat right under the window. I grabbed a bottle of water out of it and took a few sips. That was when I noticed someone standing outside and looking directly at me. I froze. A second later, he ran off, and I quickly shut the drapes.

Was he watching me the entire time?

Chapter Twelve

Jill – Fall of 1998, UCSB

THE FOLLOWING MORNING, I woke with a severe case of cottonmouth. I crawled out of bed, grabbed a water bottle, and gulped. My head pounded. *Ugh, was I that drunk last night?* I washed down a couple aspirin with the last of the water. Thankfully, it was Saturday, and there were no classes I needed to sit through.

I sat on the edge of my bed and stared at Sara's bed. It hadn't been slept in, but I knew she wouldn't be back last night. I began recalling the events of the previous night. I remembered dancing with Sara. I remembered the jungle juice we'd been drinking. One was red and the other was blue, but they tasted the same. I remembered talking to a lot of boys, all equally handsome in their own way. And how could I not remember Sara and the Bodybuilder? They were playing stand-up twister in the hallway all night long.

And then I remembered what happened when I was back in my room. I popped off my bed and peeked through a crack in the drapes. *That's where he was standing.* I remembered the spot. I also remembered his blonde hair. Well, I'm pretty sure it was blonde. I tried to remember his other physical attributes, but nothing came to me. It had happened so fast.

Should I report this to campus security? Is this something that's even reported, or would I just be laughed at? I left my window open and walked around my room in a T-shirt and panties. What did I expect to happen on a campus filled with horny boys? But still, it wasn't like he was passing by, caught a glimpse, and kept walking. He stood there and watched. Probably for a while, too. Did he see me looking at myself in the mirror? I could die!

The strangest part was that I wasn't offended or angry. In fact, if I was being honest, it turned me on.

Someone—a stranger, really—watching me when I thought I was alone was definitely an invasion of my privacy. That was how I'd felt right after seeing him. But for some reason, I didn't feel the same way the following morning. Why?

On the walk to the cafeteria, I paid attention to all the blonde-haired men I saw, looking for signs of someone watching me. I hoped I would recognize him, but that was unlikely, as it had been hard to make out the details of his face. Blonde hair was all I had.

This boy was all I could think of while I ate breakfast. Was this the first time he'd watched me? Had he done it before? I couldn't tell you the number of times I'd had the drapes pulled back and the window open while I was changing clothes, coming back from a shower, or simply prancing around nude in my room. This was all done under the assumption that no one could see me, even though my window was open. If I asked Sara, she'd say it was my fault for leaving the windows open. But it never dawned on me that someone could be standing outside watching. Why would someone be walking around back there in the woods, anyway? And yet, that night, there he was, staring me down.

As far as I could tell, this wasn't an accidental peep. This had to have been planned. He was probably waiting for me to come back to my room. Who does that? And why me? There were plenty of beautiful girls living in my dorm. Was I the only one who left the drapes open?

When I returned to my dorm, I walked around the back to see if I was the lone lunatic. I saw plenty of windows with the drapes open. Clearly, I wasn't the only one. But it was daytime, and obviously, people could have their drapes open while fully clothed.

When I reached my window, I stood where I remembered the boy standing. I had a clear view of my room. He could see everything I did the night before with no obstruction. Then the obvious dawned on me. *Has he seen me when I'm alone and...? Oh God!*

Later that night, Sara left to hang out with the Bodybuilder again. She invited me to come with her, but I declined. I didn't want to be the third wheel. Plus, I had a theory I wanted to test. I wanted to find out whether my Peeping Tom was actively seeking me out or if he was just an opportunist. Could he really be there for Sara, for instance? I wanted to know if I was the one he enjoyed watching.

That night, I changed into an even skimpier T-shirt than the one I had been wearing before (it didn't cover my panties) and ditched the bra. If a show was what he wanted, I was prepared to give it to him. When it was dark enough, I pulled the drapes apart and opened the window. I had music playing, so I spent time dancing by myself, taking quick peeks out the window now and then. So far, I hadn't seen him, but that didn't mean he wasn't there. I simply carried on as if he were. I spent some time admiring myself in the mirror. I stood on my bed and pretended to adjust a poster on the wall. I did everything I could think of to give him the best views.

And then I spotted him.

Play it cool, Jill. Don't let him know you see him.

I stood on my bed and pretended to adjust the tape holding a poster up for the millionth time. But I knew that would give him a perfect view of my legs and butt.

After a few minutes, I climbed from my bed and looked in the mirror, pretending to look myself over. That way, I could watch him in the reflection without it being obvious. He moved even closer to the window, putting himself in full view. Was he unaware, or did he not care that I could easily see him? He definitely had blonde hair, and I could make out more details on his face. He was cute.

I raised my arms to stretch, causing my shirt to ride above my stomach. If he didn't get a good look at my butt before, he was getting it now. Then I slowly turned around, arms still up and my head tilted down, looking off to the side. I felt like a ballerina spinning slowly around, letting him take it all in. I slowly looked up and smiled, expecting him to run off again.

But he didn't.

So I moved on to the second part of my plan. I grabbed a piece of paper off my desk and returned to the middle of the room. I held up the piece of paper so he could see it. Written on it in large block letters was the word "Hello."

A moment later, he ran off.

The next day, I carefully eyed every blonde guy I walked past. But none seemed to be paying extra attention to me. Maybe he still wanted to remain anonymous, only revealing himself to me outside my window. He could have just walked by without so much as a glance in my direction.

After lunch, I made my way over to the campus mailroom. I opened my mailbox and saw a folded piece of yellow notepaper inside. I unfolded it, and a handwritten message was revealed. Only two words: *Hello, back.*

Chapter Thirteen

Jill – Present Day

I walked out of Ollie's room angry, confused, and worried. Angry that my son could actually be spying on people. Confused as to why he felt the need to set his camera up to take a photo every couple of minutes while he was away. And worried that maybe Ollie was experiencing some type of mental health problem that I was only now becoming aware of.

How do I deal with this?

I made my way down to the basement, where the washer and dryer were kept.

Should I call Ollie and ask him about it? He's not due back until Sunday night. Maybe it's better to wait.

I threw a load of linens into the washer and then headed back upstairs in search of Alan. I found him out on the deck with Mia. They were talking and laughing, genuinely having a good time. Lately, I had been on Alan's case to spend more time with Mia, especially since she would go to college in a year. He always spent time with Ollie. They had common interests: They both were into photography, and recently Ollie had become more interested in astronomy. Alan was happy because they could go to the local astronomy meetups together. Alan didn't have that with Mia, and I didn't want her to feel like her father favored Ollie over her—even if he did. Rather than break up their father-daughter bonding moment, I decided this conversation about Ollie could wait.

By the time I finished doing all the laundry, it was late afternoon, and Alan had already fired up the grill. Mia wanted cheeseburgers. It was apparent that she was enjoying her time with her father; she didn't even try to make any plans with her friends that night. Of course, that meant Alan's and my chances at a date night went out the window. But for this, I was totally okay with it.

Dinner with Alan and Mia went well. The cheeseburgers were delicious, and we discussed Mia's college wish list. She really had her heart set on Stanford.

"Just to play devil's advocate," Alan said, "what are your second and third choices if you don't get in?"

"Aww, Dad. Don't say that. You'll jinx it."

"I'm just saying. And you know I don't believe in jinxes."

"Well, I want to stay on the West Coast, so USC would be my second choice. But I'd be fine at Columbia, Brown, or Yale if I had to go to the East Coast."

"All excellent choices," Alan said before taking a large bite of his double cheeseburger.

"Mom, do you think I should keep this internship on my resume?"

"Why wouldn't you? Do you think it might be a problem?"

It had definitely crossed my mind. In fact, I had planned on bringing it up with Mia. I would have hated for any fallout over Errol's suicide to harm her chances with Stanford.

"Look, Mia," Alan said. "I wouldn't worry about what happened to Mr. Tiller and if it'll affect your application process. People die every day. It's not like he was super famous outside of San Francisco. I highly doubt his name would raise an eyebrow." He shrugged and said, "Fuhgeddaboudit."

I always admired how practical Alan could be. He never let drama or emotions consume him. He always kept a level head. I wished I could have given her that answer—told her to "fuhgeddaboudit."

After dinner, Alan and Mia continued their father-daughter bonding with the stars. He showed her the popular constellations, like the big dipper. The view wasn't ideal, as there was a fair amount of light pollution from the city, but she still seemed to enjoy herself.

Of course, I was antsy to have my conversation with Alan. I wanted to pull him to the side right then and there. This thing with Ollie was serious. What if the person in the apartment found out that Ollie had been taking these pictures? What if they pressed charges? And then there was the embarrassment it would bring to our family. Alan's firm was well known in town, and I was heavily involved in charity work. Oh, and Mia. Never mind Errol, *this* could actually affect her chances of getting into Stanford. This conversation had to happen soon. I was about to interrupt Alan and Mia when my cell phone rang. It was Helen.

"Hi, Jill. What are you doing? Are you busy?"

"Not really. Well, sort of... Why? What's up?"

"I wanted to talk, but it's fine if you're in the middle of something."

"What's going on?"

"I spoke with Barbara Ezra, the widow in my building."

"Yes, I remember her."

"The police questioned her about Errol's death, because she lived below him and they were interested if she heard anything that night. She didn't, but she mentioned that Errol would make strange noises."

"What kind of noises?"

"Moaning. Barbara's words, not mine."

"Like sexual moaning? Or moaning from pain?"

"I just assumed it was sexual, so I didn't press."

"Well, I guess there's nothing wrong with that."

"No, there's not. But she also overheard the police talking while they were on Errol's balcony. She said they thought it was suicide."

"Well, yeah. I think we all think that's the reason."

"I bet financial problems drove him to do this."

"Helen, why are you so interested in Errol and this investigation?"

"I don't know. I mean, it happened in my building. And it's not like I had this experience before."

"Well, if it was financial trouble, that could also open the door to something else."

Helen drew a deep breath. "I was thinking the same thing. What if Errol was murdered? You know, like thrown over the balcony."

As soon as Helen said that, the image of that falling body popped into my mind. Was it falling because it had been thrown? A murder investigation could gain more attention in the news. That could be news that made its way out of San Francisco to the Stanford community.

"Helen, I have something to tell you."

"What is it?"

"I think I saw Errol fall."

"What?"

I went ahead and explained to Helen how I had looked through the telescope while I was waiting for Alan to come home.

"Are you serious? Are you sure it was Errol? Wait, what am I saying? Of course, it was Errol. I can't believe it. What are the odds?"

"I know, right? At first, I thought it was my imagination, or I had dust in my eye. But the more I think about it, the surer I am that I saw Errol falling."

"Does Alan know?"

"Yes. I told him because I thought we should tell the police."

"What did he say?"

"You know Alan, sometimes he can come across as indifferent. He told me not to worry about it, because all I saw was a falling body, and I didn't see how Errol fell or why. He said that's what the police would be interested in."

"But did you? Did you see him fall from his balcony?"

I thought about Helen's question. My field of view had included Errol's balcony. Still, I didn't notice a body until midway through the frame. I saw it leave my view, and that was when I pulled away from the telescope.

"Um, now that I think about it...I'm not exactly sure."

"What do you mean you're not sure? Jill, this is important. You might have seen whether or not he jumped on his own or whether someone forced him off."

Alan and I had agreed that I shouldn't tell anyone about this, and here I was blabbing about it to Helen. Now, suddenly, there was a chance I might know exactly what happened.

"Look, I promised Alan I wouldn't say anything, so if it comes up while the three of us are together, I never said anything."

"What are you talking about? The three of us are rarely all together."

"I'm just saying."

"I know, but I'm serious, Jill. You might be the one person who knows exactly what happened to Errol. You might hold the key to naming the person who killed Errol."

"I know, but I'm not one hundred percent sure. I drank two

bottles of wine. I mean, isn't that something that would make me not a credible witness?"

"Only if you tell them you drank two bottles. Personally, I'd keep that to myself. People will start to think you're an alcoholic."

"I'm not an alcoholic!" I whisper-shouted into the phone.

"I'm kidding, Jill. Relax... You're only an alcoholic if you were drinking alone."

"Helen, I'm not—"

"I'm kidding," she said as she laughed.

"It's not funny."

"I'm sorry. I won't say another word about all the wine you had."

"What should I do?"

"You need to think hard about that moment and determine if you saw Errol leave his balcony."

"But do I really need to? It's not like anyone knows what I saw. I could keep quiet like Alan wants, and let this situation play out."

"Is that what you want to do?"

"I mean, why would I want to drag myself and my family into this mess with Errol's death if I don't have to? It seems sort of stupid, right?"

"Yeah, I suppose. Maybe it's better if you keep your mouth shut. It's better to avoid this entire Errol mess."

After I hung up with Helen, I checked on Alan and Mia. They'd left the deck and gone up to the entertainment room.

"Hey, you're just in time," Alan said. "We're getting ready to watch *The Sound of Music*. It's been a while since we did this as a family. I mean, Ollie's not here, but Mia is."

"Yeah, Mom. Join us. I'm the important child, anyway." Mia grinned.

Settling in with my family and watching a movie sounded like the perfect thing to take my mind off the conversation I'd just had with Helen and this whole thing with Ollie. Oh, who was I kidding? I would need more than Julie's singing to stop my overthinking.

Chapter Fourteen

Helen

I ended the call with Jill in a state of disbelief. The only reason I'd called and brought up the investigation into Errol's death was so that Jill could tell me I was overthinking. But that wasn't what happened. Now everything felt worse.

I plopped down on my sofa and tilted my head back. I finally had my shit together in life, money in the bank, and a thriving online business. It was what I'd always wanted. And now this thing with Errol could put it all in jeopardy. *That bastard!*

I knew if the police started to seriously treat Errol's death as murder, they would find out about his connections with me. It was inevitable; I couldn't cover it up completely.

Should I go on the offensive?

Volunteering information to those detectives might be the right move. But what would be my reason for contacting them out of the blue? Why would I tell them I had a relationship with Errol? Wasn't that something someone offered up because they were being questioned? I realized I was in the same situation as Jill, with her seeing Errol fall. Why volunteer that information if the police weren't asking for it? It wasn't like the police put out a statement asking for the public's help. Sometimes they'd set up a tip hotline, but that hadn't been done as far as I knew.

Maybe I needed to prepare myself for questioning, so I didn't end up blabbing.

I sat at my desk, took a notepad, and wrote down the heading:

<u>Questions I Will Be Asked</u>

- Do you know Errol, and if so, how well do you know him?

As I stared at the paper, I realized that was the only question they needed to ask. How I met Errol and the nature of our relationship could have led to his death. They'd think I had a motive, I'd become a suspect, and then I'd be screwed.

Wait a minute, Helen. Let's not freak out. Think about how Alan would handle this situation. He's pragmatic and good at problem-solving. He told Jill not to offer up any information unless she was asked. That's what a lawyer would advise. They'd say to keep my mouth shut. Why the hell am I thinking about what to tell them?

I decided my best way forward was to copy Jill and keep my quiet. But it couldn't hurt to prepare an answer.

Maybe the plan could be to give them partial truths, like literally answer a question without elaborating or offering anything else unless they directly ask for specifics. Or better yet, focus on how Errol and I met and our relationship at that time. Could I live with that? I think so. Would that answer satisfy them? I think it might. Because if they focus on the money angle and keep digging, I'm done.

Chapter Fifteen

SFPD

SOKOLOV AND BENNIE returned to the station after visiting Tiller & Associates. They'd been interviewing people since the crack of dawn and wanted to compile their thoughts on everything they'd learned so far.

Bennie pulled a rolling bulletin board over to their desks and began pinning up a list of what they knew.

- Tiller's company is having financial difficulties.
- His partners wanted him out.
- Signs of excessive drinking and drug use.
- Tiller's administrative assistant noticed a change in his behavior.

"This is all pointing to suicide," Bennie said.

"What about the missing dog?"

"If he was putting his affairs in order, it makes sense to give the dog away."

Just then, Guillermo appeared.

"Hey, I got more findings for you."

"Good or bad?" Sokolov asked.

"Mostly bad, but let's start off with a positive. Of all the prints we lifted from the apartment, we were only able to match one besides the victim. Does the name Darrel Knight ring a bell?"

"Yeah, he's the assistant super at the building."

"Well, he was in the apartment and held one of the glasses. So that places him in the apartment that night. Here's a printout of his rap sheet." Guillermo handed Sokolov a piece of paper.

"Theft, assault, drug possession, resisting arrest, disorderly conduct, vandalism," Sokolov read. "It's a long rap sheet, but nothing crazy."

"Did a year in lockup. He's been free and clean for the past three years," Bennie said. "I bet this is why he lied to us. I'm guessing his employer doesn't know he did time."

"We need to find out what his story is with Tiller."

"That's not all," Guillermo cut in. "Knight also handled the bag of cocaine. So either he partook in the partying, or he delivered the goods. But being that he handled a glass, there's a chance he did both."

"When we questioned him earlier, he told us he barely knew the guy," Bennie said.

"The other two sets of prints were not on any of the glasses or bottles of alcohol or anywhere near the party scene. One pair was found all over the bedroom and attached bathroom. The other was picked up on the island in the kitchen."

"So he had sex with one and a conversation with the other," Sokolov said. "What else you got?"

"Moving on to the hair I collected. We confirmed, one is canine. I was even able to get it down to the breed. The hair is of a pug."

"We've heard from three people that Tiller had a pug."

"If he did, it's gone now. The other strands of hair were long and chemically treated, which suggests female. They were missing the root, so DNA analysis isn't possible. But I'm guessing if Tiller had guests that night, they were female. Now, if you can figure out who those two other prints belong to, you can see if their hair matches what we have."

Guillermo looked at what Bennie had pinned to the board and nodded. "Toxicology report came back with alcohol and high levels of cocaine in Tiller's system. He was loaded when he went over that balcony. Honestly, there's a good chance he went over by accident. That's all I got for now. If anything else comes up, I'll let you know."

"It looks like Knight was Tiller's cocaine connection," Bennie said after Guillermo left.

"Yeah, he delivers the bag and sticks around for a taste. The two continue to party, and then they have a falling out for some reason. A push becomes a shove, and Tiller goes over the railing."

"Could be accidental or on purpose," Bennie said.

"Either way, Tiller's death is starting to look less like suicide and more like murder."

Chapter Sixteen

Jill

IT WAS ten when we finished the movie. Mia was eager to get back on her phone with her friends and promptly headed to her bedroom. That allowed Alan and me to talk. I tapped his shoulder.

"We have to talk about something."

"Sure, what's on your mind?"

"Not here. Follow me."

We headed to Ollie's room, and I pointed at his camera set. "Every few minutes, that camera is taking a picture automatically."

"Huh?"

"Wait and listen."

A moment later, the camera shutter went off, and the LCD screen on the back of the camera lit up briefly. Alan walked over to the camera and examined it.

"He's using an intervalometer...my intervalometer."

"What's that?"

Alan held up some device in his hand that was attached to the camera by a small cord. "This. It basically programs the camera to automatically snap a photo. This is how he's capturing all these photos without actually being here. When he asked me for it, I thought he had plans to photograph the stars. This is typical in astronomy photography."

Alan bent down and peered through the viewfinder. "The apartment building. No surprise there."

He pressed a few buttons, the LCD screen came to life, and he began to scroll through the photos the camera had taken. They were all of the living room of an apartment.

"If he was hoping to capture the person living there, he's out of luck. All of the photos are of an empty living room."

Alan continued to scroll.

"Ah, here we go. These photos are from Thursday."

Alan moved off to the side, and I moved in for a closer look. The photos were of a blonde woman.

"Who is that?" I asked.

"Beats me, but Ollie seems to be infatuated with her."

She clearly wasn't a minor, which made me feel a bit better, but not totally. She was also fully clothed. But I was sure those weren't the photos Ollie was after.

"I can't believe our son is spying on that woman. What is wrong with him? Doesn't he know this is against the law?"

"Well, wait a minute. I know it doesn't look good, but let's give him the benefit of the doubt until we hear his side."

"Oh, come on, Alan. What do you think he's doing? He wants sexy photos of that woman."

"I'm not arguing with that. All I'm saying is let's give him a chance to tell his side of the story."

"Should we call him now? Is it too late?"

"I think this would be a better conversation to have with him when he returns home. This is a private matter. Right now, he might be surrounded by a bunch of people."

"You're right, but...doesn't it worry you? You seem so...I don't know, relaxed about it. He's invading that woman's privacy. He could be passing these photos on to his friends, or God forbid, uploading them to the internet."

Alan put his arm around me, pulled me in, and kissed me on top of my head. "Hey, I get it. This is serious, and we'll deal with it appropriately if that's what he's doing. But right now, we only have half the story. We need the other half."

"I know. It's just that I'm worried. This woman could press charges."

"First off, we don't know this woman. Maybe Ollie doesn't even know this woman. It could be completely random. Secondly, how would she even know what was happening unless we told her?"

"Well, what if Ollie did something dumb, like pass the photos around? If someone uploads one to the internet, it's forever, you know."

"I know. But like I said, let's wait until we hear what Ollie has to say. No sense in letting our imaginations run wild and getting worked up over it."

I opened my mouth to say something but shut it quickly.

"What?"

"It's nothing."

"Hey, no secrets, right?"

He was so calm about this that it made me question whether he cared.

"I feel like you aren't taking this seriously. Our son is watching a woman. Wait, strike that. He's trying to capture photographs of a naked woman. You know it as well as I do."

"Our son is sixteen. His hormones are raging. I'm sure he's jerked off to her already."

"Eeewww, Alan."

"What do you think teenage boys do? I probably jerked off five times a day when I was that age."

"But why can't he just look at porn on his laptop or something? Those people are paid professionals. They know what is happening to their videos and pictures."

"I don't know. Like I said, we need to hear Ollie's side."

"Alan, don't get mad when I ask you this, but I need to know. Were you aware that Ollie was doing this with your intervalometer?"

"Of course not."

"But did you know he was looking at that woman? Tell me the truth, Alan."

"No, Jill. I didn't know. But I'm beginning to think having this conversation is pointless, because it looks like you've made up your mind. Think what you want, but I didn't put the kid up to this."

"It's just that..."

"It's just that what, Jill? Go on, say what's on your mind."

"It's your hobby..."

"You mean 'our hobby.'"

Chapter Seventeen

Jill – Fall of 1998, UCSB

Two months had passed, and I'd put on numerous shows during that time. I don't know precisely how many my admirer saw, because I didn't always see him. But that didn't mean he wasn't watching.

Sara and I always went out together on Friday nights. That was our thing. But on Saturdays, she went out on dates. So I had the room to myself, and Saturdays became my performance night. In my head, that was exactly what I was doing for my audience of one.

At first, it was more of what I had done the first time. I'd dress in something sexy and pretend to do mundane things in my room, like reading, cleaning, or even doing homework. But after a while, I'd become a little braver. And to be honest, I thought if I kept doing those same things repeatedly, he'd get bored and stop watching.

So I started dancing. Not bouncing around like a girl from a teen movie, but *moving*, seductively. I channeled a lot of Madonna back then. I also bought outfits especially for those nights. Sometimes I wore fishnet stockings with a halter dress. Sometimes, it was a bikini with body paint and blacklight. Not only did the thought of someone watching turn me on, the creativity involved with planning my Saturday performances was exhilarating, too.

I found myself spending more and more time on what I would wear and do. It was like I finally had an opportunity to express myself without fear. Growing up, I'd always been shy and avoided the spotlight, mostly because I didn't think I deserved it. But with my admirer, it was different. He wasn't judging or commenting. There were no awkward stares, no snickering or finger-pointing. He simply enjoyed me and all that I had to give. And I freaking loved that. We hadn't even spoken a single word to each other, yet he made me feel special.

But I finally got to the point where I wanted to—strike that, I *had* to meet this man who empowered me to be me. I know it's crazy. Most women would consider this man perverted, scream "Ewwww!" and draw the curtains before reporting him to campus police. Nowadays, he would have been videoed, posted to social media, and canceled. And I get it. Under normal circumstances, I would have done the same. But for some stupid reason, I didn't find him cringey or perverted. It wasn't like he stood there masturbating. And I was never nude or doing anything vulgar. But there was definitely sexual energy in the air. I found him to be mysterious, exciting, and a little dangerous.

During this time, we also continued our note exchanges. Nothing heavy. I'd hold a sign saying "Hey there" or "Enjoy." He'd always answer by leaving a message in my campus mail-box, something like "Thank you" or "You rock!" It was our special way of communicating.

One Saturday night, I dressed as Princess Leia in that gold bikini from the Jabba the Hutt scene. I wasn't sure if he was a sci-fi nut, but he was a guy, and I was pretty sure he'd want to see me in that outfit. Anyway, I had decided this was the night

I'd make a move to meet my admirer. I'd grown tired of anxiously looking at every blonde guy I passed or spoke to on campus. We needed to meet, even if it was for only ten minutes. I wanted to see him up close, hear his voice, and look into his eyes. I wasn't looking to necessarily change our relationship. I wanted to continue what we had, but I also wanted a little more from him.

My handwritten sign that night was an invitation to meet. I wasn't expecting an answer right then and there. I figured he'd place a message in my mailbox the following day. I usually checked my mail after lunch. Waiting seemed like an eternity, and I had difficulty concentrating on my class lectures. When lunch rolled around, I ate a tuna sandwich and a small bowl of tomato soup as quickly as possible before hurrying to the mailroom.

I put my key into the lock of my mailbox, turned the knob, and pulled the small door open. Inside, I recognized the yellow lined paper he always used. My heart jumped, and warmth spread out across my chest. My hand shook with anticipation as I retrieved the paper. I slowly unfolded it; he always folded the paper in fours. I looked around quickly to make sure no one was near me. With the coast clear, I flattened it out and read what he had written: *Tonight, meet me in the quad at 9 p.m.*

You would have thought I'd just gotten asked out to my senior prom by the most popular boy in school with the way my heart fluttered. I reread the message to be sure I'd read it right the first time. I had. I would finally meet my admirer.

If I thought waiting until after lunch was hard, waiting until nine o'clock that night would feel like an eternity. I read the message once more. There was no mention of the word "date," so this meeting could be a quick wave with a "nice to meet you" and then be over. I hoped it wouldn't be, because I had a million questions I wanted to ask him. But I didn't want to come across like a psych student working on my dissertation. I also wanted him to know that I was totally okay with our actions, no judgments.

I needed to prioritize my questions from most important to least. I had to prepare as if this meeting would be over in ten minutes. What was the one question I wanted to ask him? Would it be, "Why do you watch me?" How about, "When did it start?" Or, "Is it sexual for you?"

Of course, there were the typical questions I would ask: "What's your name?" "What are you studying?" "Where are you from?" I'd be happy to answer any of his questions. There was nothing I wanted to hide from him. He made me feel comfortable, and I trusted him, even though we'd never met.

When I was eight years old, I had gotten a pen pal through a program at my school. It was a totally random match. If we wanted to participate, we didn't have the option to choose someone. I ended up with Timothy, a boy a year older than me who lived across the country in Connecticut. I can't recall the town. But I knew there was never a chance that we would ever meet while I was living in Tiburon, California. So I didn't really care what I wrote in my letters. I'd ramble on about all sorts of things happening in my life, school, with my family. It felt good to talk without worrying whether what I said was wrong or right.

Timothy wasn't much of a writer. He'd always answer with a paragraph telling me about his day. Then he'd include some drawings. Sometimes it was a superhero, or sometimes it was a shark. I recalled them being really good. I'd even hung a few on my bedroom wall. But our pen pal relationship lasted for the school year, and that was it. We stopped writing.

I never had a relationship like that one again, one where I could be totally open, without any judgments. That is, until I met my admirer.

After I finished my classes, I spent the rest of the afternoon trying on a bunch of different outfits. I was about to meet my admirer in a totally different setting. I wasn't going as Jill, the performer. I was showing up as Jill, the ordinary university student. He needed to see this side of me that wasn't in character.

At 8:45 p.m., I took one last look at myself in the mirror. I decided on blue jeans, a cute top, and sneakers. I had pulled my hair back into a ponytail and wore lipstick and a little blush. I hoped he was ready for the real Jill.

Sara wasn't in our room, which was perfect, because I didn't feel like explaining what I was up to. Too much backstory was needed for her to fully appreciate the situation and not yell at me for letting someone watch me through the window. She probably would have prevented me from meeting this man, or insisted on coming with me.

The UCSB quad was a large paved area with benches. It was dotted with plots of small trees. Off to the side was a small pond with water lilies and a fountain. A fair number of people were hanging out in the quad that night. Part of me wished he had selected a place that wasn't so crowded. But the upside was, if our meeting didn't go well and he turned out to be a crazy killer, I'd have a whole bunch of witnesses.

I scanned the benches first but didn't see a blonde man who looked like him. I looked over at the pond, where people sat on the concrete perimeter encircling it. That was when I spotted a man with blonde hair looking straight at me. He had a smile on his face. A second later, he waved at me.

I walked over to him, matching his smile. He stood just as I arrived. He was much taller than I thought he would be. He had light blue eyes, a lovely jawline, and wore torn jeans and a UCSB sweater.

He stuck his hand out. "It's nice to meet you. My name is Alan."

Chapter Eighteen

Jill – Present Day

"I can't believe you're trying to blame this on me," Alan said.

"I'm just pointing out the elephant in the room. No secrets, right?"

Alan closed Ollie's bedroom door. "Let's keep our voices down. There's no need for Mia to overhear."

I folded my arms across my chest. "Alan, I'm not trying to attack you. I'm just throwing out ideas as to why Ollie might be doing this. I mean, maybe it's something that can be passed down."

"You think my hobby has been passed down to Ollie like a hereditary trait? Sheesh, Jill."

"Do you know if it can or can't?"

I knew that look on Alan's face, the one where he squinted and this weird crinkle formed between his eyebrows. It was the look of "What is this crazy woman talking about?"

"I'm not crazy," I said. "I'm brainstorming."

"I don't know if it can be passed down. And if it can be, then you can't blame me. That means I had no control over it. You can only blame me if it's a learned behavior. And I didn't teach Ollie this, nor have I ever discussed this topic with him or even hinted at it. All of our discussions about photography and astronomy were normal. You have to believe me on this, Jill. You do believe me, right?"

"Of course, I believe you."

I had about five percent of doubt at the moment, but ultimately, I always believed Alan.

"Do you think he knows about us?" I asked.

"You mean what we do?" Alan took a moment to think. "I don't think so. We're pretty good about keeping it from the kids."

"Maybe he snooped around our bedroom. Do you keep any files?"

"Let's continue this conversation in our bedroom," Alan said in a lowered voice. "I'm worried Mia might be able to hear us through the wall."

We left Ollie's room and went upstairs. Alan closed our bedroom door behind him.

"Answer my question," I said. "Do you keep any of it?"

He's hesitating. He never hesitates.

"I kept some of it."

I threw my arms up in the air. "Alan! Why are you keeping it? I thought you deleted it all when we were finished."

"I got rid of most of it! But I kept some."

"Show me. I want to see what you're keeping."

"It's nothing, Jill. Don't worry about it. You know me, it's not sexual, and I'm not lusting over anyone. I only watch."

Yes, I married a Peeping Tom. Alan hated that term, so I never used it around him. He also didn't believe "voyeur" suited him; he said that entails a sexual element. Alan preferred to call it "watching."

"Do you know who lives in the apartment Ollie is photographing?" I continued my line of questioning.

"That I don't know, but like you, I'm eager to find out who the mystery person is."

Alan opened a case that held his most prized telescope—it looked like roller luggage. Inside was a twenty-thousand-dollar telescope. It wasn't one of those telescopes that had a skinny optical tube. This one was short, fat, and resembled a floodlight on a tripod. It had a powerful lens, which made looking at the stars amazing. I could only imagine if I had looked through this telescope when Errol fell, I might have seen the expression on his face.

Alan set up the telescope inside our bedroom and parted the drapes. He then peered through the lens viewer.

"Fourteenth floor, right?" he asked.

"That's right, the second apartment from the right," I said.

"Got it. The curtains are still open, but no one's home." He looked back at me. "Come take a look."

I bent down and took a peek. "Wow, I can make out the photographs hanging on her wall. This is so much better than Ollie's lens."

"Thirty K for this telescope."

I looked up at him. "You told me twenty."

"I upgraded," he said with a shrug. "We'll keep it focused on the apartment. There's a chance we can find out more about this woman before Ollie gets back from his trip."

I moved away from the telescope and sat on the edge of our bed.

"What's wrong?" Alan asked.

"I'm worried about Ollie. He's not like you. What if he can't control his urges? What if this morphs into something more, like stalking? It's like a...a gateway drug. Stalking leads to kidnapping, which leads to killing. I don't want my son to be a serial killer."

Alan took a seat next to me and put a comforting arm

around me. "He's not turning into a serial killer. That shit starts with killing animals. Well, he does like to fish..."

"Alan!"

"I'm joking. I'm sorry. Look, Ollie is our son. We won't let anything bad happen, even if it means sending him to a therapist. But let's try not to blow this up with our imaginations. We have to give Ollie the benefit of the doubt."

Chapter Nineteen

Jill – Eighteen months before

I HAD FALLEN COMPLETELY in love with the house when I first looked at it. I just knew we had to have it. At the time, we were living in an apartment that was roomy enough for Alan, me, and the kids, but it was nothing like living in a good house. Alan's career was solid at the time, and we felt like the moment was right to upgrade. We'd been looking for something in the city for the past six months, and we'd come across many great choices, mostly charming Victorians. In fact, we were ready to make an offer on one when our realtor told us about a home that had just come onto the market with a killer view of the bay. We made a generous offer above asking and closed on our new home in a week.

Alan had always told me he would defer to me on which house we would purchase. He'd told me, "I want you and the kids to be happy." Of course, I did make sure he loved the house, as well. He'd thought it was the best we'd looked at and wanted it as much as I did. That was reassuring; this was a large purchase, and it was important we were both on the same page.

My only complaint had been the building in the middle of our view, the one I called the "Middle Finger." That's what it was doing to me every day I stood on the deck and looked out at the bay: giving me the middle finger.

It didn't seem to bother Alan. At first, I didn't question why, because, at the time, I had forgotten entirely about his hobby. But of course, it wouldn't bother him. It was the ideal situation: an unobstructed view of more than twenty individual apartments.

He had his setup complete within a month of moving into the house. Alan had bought a high-end telescope and somehow hooked it up to the flat-screen we kept in our bedroom. He also had a remote that allowed him to point the telescope wherever he wanted, zoom in and out, and adjust the focus. At the same time, he would lie comfortably on our bed. I'd lie right next to him, reading, while he watched. It didn't take long before I was watching. I can't explain it, but somehow it became addicting. It was like watching a real-life reality show.

Alan stood naked at the foot of our bed, eating a slice of pizza. The kids were visiting their grandparents for the weekend, so Alan and I had the house all to ourselves. We were like a couple of teenagers. We spent almost all of that time in the house, having sex, smoking pot, and eating delivery, all while watching our neighbors in the building across the way.

"Shall we see what the Mortons are up to? Or maybe Pest Guy," he said as he chomped on the crust.

Since we didn't know these people's real names, we gave them fake ones. The Mortons were an elderly couple. The husband was always in the living room watching television, and his wife was always yelling at him from the kitchen. Pest Guy always seemed to be hunting down bugs in his place.

I liked that it was our thing, much like when Alan and I first met. First, it was him watching me through my window. Now, we watched together.

When I had met Alan back at UCSB, he did his best to

explain why he did what he did. He made it clear from the beginning that it wasn't sexual, even when he was watching me dance around my room half-naked. He'd said I was the most beautiful woman he'd ever seen, but he didn't watch to get his rocks off. He watched to admire my beauty and happy-go-lucky way. Or so he said.

So far, none of the watching we did together was sexual. We got enjoyment out of seeing people living their ordinary lives. I was fine with that. And to be honest, at the time, I didn't see how anything problematic could arise from our hobby.

Chapter Twenty

Ollie Pittman – Present Day

It was totally turning out to be an awesome weekend. My best friend, Grant, invited me to go camping and fishing with him and his dad. We were in the Sierra Nevada, a mountain range about a three-hour drive from San Francisco. That whole place is national park land. Yosemite National Park is the most popular, but we were camping in the nearby Stanislaus National Forest. The crowds there weren't as crazy as they were in Yosemite. In fact, there was no one around our campsite.

My dad isn't a big fan of outdoor stuff, aside from looking at the stars. I got into it because I joined the Cub Scouts when I was younger. That's how I met Grant. We were the same age and both new to Cub Scouts, so we bonded and have remained friends ever since.

My family used to live in Noe Valley, far from where Grant lived in the North Beach neighborhood of San Francisco, so we didn't see each other as much as we would have liked. But two years ago, my parents moved us to Nob Hill. That put me a short bike ride away from Grant, and we even went to the same school.

"Man, I'm beat," Grant said as we walked back to our tent. "But my mind doesn't want to go to sleep."

"I know. I feel the same way. I don't want to waste any part of this weekend."

Grant's dad, Mr. Walker, was content to sit around the campfire and drink beers, listening to old music. It was boring, and we couldn't drink, so Grant and I decided to chill in our tent.

It had taken us three hours to drive out to the Sierras, but Grant's and my parents let us skip school on Friday to get a head start on our trip. We left at six in the morning and arrived at nine. We quickly set up our campsite and hit the river for some fishing. Since it was September, there was no limit on the number of brown trout we could catch, so long as they were bigger than fourteen inches. Altogether, we reeled in ten of them. We grilled a bunch for lunch and saved the rest for dinner. We spent the afternoon hiking and checking out the wildlife. The highlight was a black bear sighting. We yelled and waved our arms around, and it ran off pretty quickly. Cell service in the forest was nonexistent, so I turned my phone off. After all, we had taken the trip to escape civilization, not tap into it.

Grant zipped up the tent while I lay down on my sleeping bag. It was only ten at night, but I was tired after the day we'd had. I grabbed my phone, switched it on, and to my surprise, I had one bar.

"Hey, my internet's working. Grant, check your phone and see if you got it, too," I said.

It took forever for my social media to load, but when it did, I saw that everyone was talking about Errol Tiller's death.

"Grant, are you seeing this?" I asked.

"Yeah, I'm reading a couple of posts now. They're saying he committed suicide."

"I can't believe it."

I didn't know Mr. Tiller personally, but my sister had done an internship for his company over the summer.

"This is so awesome. I hated that son of a bitch," Grant said.

Grant's family lived in the same building as Mr. Tiller, so I also heard about him from Grant from time to time.

"I can't believe it worked," Grant said.

"Do you really think that's the reason?"

"Why not? Either way, that bastard is dead, and I'm psyched about it."

"Do you think your Dad knows about this?" I asked.

"Probably not. I mean, we only found out just now."

"No, I mean about the other thing?"

Grant shook his head. "No, and I'm glad he doesn't know. It would cause problems in our family, and my Mom has already caused enough."

"Are you still ignoring her?"

"I was, but now that Mr. Tiller's dead, I don't feel that angry."

Grant had been in a funk for the last two months because of what his mother did. I didn't blame him. I would have felt the same way if I were in his shoes. Sometimes I wish I never saw what I saw. Or I wished I'd never told Grant. But I had to. He was my best friend. If the situation were reversed, I would want to know.

"Are you telling your Dad about Mr. Tiller's death?" I asked.

"Nah, I don't see the point. He'll find out eventually, since we live in the same building. At least I won't have to see my Dad saying 'hello' to that bastard when he passes him in the lobby. I hated it. Mr. Tiller would smile and wave like he did nothing wrong. To hell with him. The world is better without him."

That may have been true. I wasn't about to judge Grant for his animosity toward the man.

"He should have stayed away. It's totally his fault," Grant said.

"Damn right."

"We did the right thing, Ollie."

"Did we?"

"Of course. Mr. Tiller is dead."

Chapter Twenty-One

Darrel Knight

IT WAS A SUNDAY MORNING, and I was looking forward chilling with my wife and baby boy. Then, I got a call from Detective Sokolov asking me to come in and answer questions. I couldn't believe the crap these detectives were pulling. And it was my day off. I told them we could meet at the building on Monday morning and that I was busy. Detective Sokolov suggested he could stop by my place. The last thing I wanted was for the police to question me in front of my wife. She was already stressing about money; she didn't need this, too. So I went.

I knew this meeting was bullshit. The detective said he had a few more questions about Mr. Tiller, but I had already told them everything I knew about the guy. They tripping over nothing.

I knew the real reason they were calling me in. They ran my name and found out I had a rap sheet. So what? I'd been clean for the past three years and was a solid worker. People deserve second chances in life. Man, I even told them my wife and I just had a baby. I had responsibilities now. The old Darrel was in the past.

I parked my car in a garage about a block from the police station—of course, I had to pay for parking, on top of everything else. My wife and I were on a tight budget, and the last thing I needed was a stupid expense like paying for parking in the city.

"I'm here to see Detective Sokolov," I said to the desk officer.

"Have a seat," he said.

I spotted Detective Sokolov walking toward me a few moments later.

"Mr. Knight. I appreciate you coming in. Follow me. I have an interview room where we can talk privately."

The other detective from the day before caught up with us. We entered an interrogation room.

"You remember Detective Bennie, right?"

"Yeah, sure."

I took a seat on one side of the table, and they sat on the other.

"So, what's this about?" I asked.

Detective Sokolov removed a pen from his jacket. "We needed some clarification on your relationship with Mr. Tiller."

"What's to know? I'm a maintenance guy. I fix things for the residents in the building. Sometimes it's him, and sometimes it's not."

He flipped through a small notepad. "You told us the last time you saw Mr. Tiller was last month."

"Yeah, that's right."

Detective Bennie opened a folder he'd been carrying and placed a photograph on the table.

"Does this glass look familiar to you?" Detective Sokolov asked.

"Looks like any other glass."

"This glass was on the coffee table in Mr. Tiller's apartment."

"So?"

"Well, your fingerprints are on it. Does it seem familiar now?"

Shit!

I watched Detective Bennie place another photograph on the table: a liquor bottle.

"Your prints were also on this bottle. Residue liquor from that bottle was found in the glass. Does that help your recollection?"

"Man, how do you know those are my prints?"

Detective Bennie placed another piece of paper on the table.

"We know you have a record and were incarcerated for a year, Darrel," Detective Bennie said. "Your prints are on file."

I shook my head. "Man, I didn't do anything. If you think I had something to do with Mr. Tiller's death, you're wrong."

"Help us understand," Detective Sokolov said. "And this time, don't lie to us. Because we will find out."

"All right, so I was there that night. I had a drink. Nothing wrong with that."

"No, there isn't," Detective Sokolov said.

Detective Bennie opened the folder again.

"What the hell? You got another damn photo?"

"There was cocaine on that same coffee table," Detective Bennie said. "It came in this baggie. Your prints are on the baggie."

"You guys are setting me up. You're making it look bad."

"How should it look?" Detective Sokolov asked. "Mr. Knight, we know you have a newborn. The last thing you need is any problems with the law. So help us understand."

I let out a long breath as I shook my head. "Every now and then, I would score coke for Mr. Tiller. I mean, he ain't exactly the kind of guy that'll roll up on a street corner and buy the stuff himself. So when he asked if I knew where to score some, I told him I did, but I would only buy grams. I wasn't playing around with anything bigger than that. I had a kid on the way. Anyway, I thought I could put a mark on it and make some easy money on the side."

"I can understand that," Detective Sokolov said.

"Are you popping me for possession?"

"Relax, we work homicide. This doesn't interest us. So, this side action—roughly how long had you been scoring for Mr. Tiller, and how often?"

"I would say he approached me about six, maybe seven months ago. At first, it was once every couple of weeks, then it was once every week. Next thing you know, this guy wants deliveries twice a week."

"So, what caused the problem?" Detective Sokolov asked.

"What problem?"

"You know, the reason you kept calling Mr. Tiller at his office. We have a record of you calling him daily, multiple times. A person only calls like that when there's an urgent problem that needs to be dealt with."

"Man, so look, everything was fine. And then, one day, Mr. Tiller wants a delivery but asks me to cover for him. He says he doesn't have cash on him. I say 'cool,' because this guy is rich. He's good for it. But the guy didn't pay me the next day like he was supposed to. A few days later, he asks for another delivery and gives me some bull about not having time to go to the bank. Next thing you know, the guy is avoiding me over two large. That's nothing for him, but it's a lot for me."

"Did you take the coke on credit?"

"Yeah, of course. The dealer trusted me, but then I had him calling me every day, wanting his money. I finally got a cousin of mine to hook me up so I could pay off the dealer. But I still needed Mr. Tiller to pay up."

"And that's why you started calling him at the office?"

"Yeah, I swear that's the truth."

"On Friday, did you visit Mr. Tiller to collect or drop off another delivery?"

"Both. He said he'd pay me when I got there. But man, he only paid me eighteen hundred. He still owed two hundred plus another three hundred for the bag I had just brought. He promised on Monday he would settle everything."

"Did you believe him?"

"No...but man, what was I supposed to do? I needed that money, and I knew he'd eventually get it. But I told him I couldn't score for him no more because the dealer had cut me off."

"What time did you arrive at Mr. Tiller's apartment, and how long were you there?"

"I'd say it was around seven. I left work, made the score, and came right back. I talked some bullshit with him, had a drink, and bounced."

"And he was alone?"

"Yeah."

"Have you ever seen anyone there with Mr. Tiller while he was partying?"

"Nah, man, normally I hand him the bag at the door. I don't want to go inside and get all up in his business. But that night, he pulled me inside."

"Was he already under the influence?"

"Man, the guy was as high as a kite. A little paranoid if you ask me—like a crackhead, but he wasn't that far gone."

"Did he mention anything about having someone over or expecting someone else?"

I shook my head. "We had no time to talk. I downed that drink and left. I swear."

"Here's the problem, Darrel. There's no proof that you had one drink and left," Detective Sokolov said. "Your criminal record shows you've been arrested for assault multiple times. That leads me to believe you have a temper. Maybe things got heated between you two, and there was some pushing and shoving, and then Mr. Tiller went over the railing."

"That's bullshit! I ain't killed Mr. Tiller. You be putting words in my mouth. Those assault charges, that's the old Darrel. The new Darrel ain't trying to go back to jail. I got a kid now."

"I don't know what to tell you. Right now, you're the last person to see Mr. Tiller alive."

"Wait, hold up. I just remembered something."

"What's that?"

"I've seen Peggy, the building manager, go into his apartment multiple times."

"Elaborate on that."

"I seen her take the elevator and go up to his floor."

"That doesn't mean she went into his apartment. It just proves the elevator went to his floor."

"Okay, well check this. One day I had to replace light bulbs in the stairwell. I was on Mr. Tiller's floor, and as I came out of the stairwell, I see Peggy come out of his apartment. She was giggling, and her hair was all messed up. If you ask me, it looked like Mr. Tiller just got done pounding the punnani pavement."

"Did you see her go into his apartment Friday night?"

"No, but I passed her on the way out of the building when I came back with Mr. Tiller's delivery. She always wears really strong perfume. You know when she's been around. When I got off on his floor, I smelled it. Now, based on what I saw before, there ain't no way she went up there for some building business. Those two got something going on. I wasn't the only one in that apartment the night he died."

Chapter Twenty-Two

Jill

I woke up in a foul mood, mainly because I had had trouble sleeping all night. My mind couldn't stop going over and over what Ollie had done. And it irritated me even more that Alan slept soundly. How could he be so relaxed about the situation? Our son set up a camera to take pictures of an apartment every few minutes. What teenager does something like that? It wasn't like Ollie was on an FBI stakeout.

Twice I came close to waking Alan to continue our conversation. Still, I knew it would only make the situation between us worse. He might have been right about not discussing this until Ollie got home, but I also had a good point about Alan's hobby. What if, somehow, some way, Ollie found out what he did?

Of course, I was a part of it. Was I ashamed of that? I wasn't before; it was just fun. But things were different this time, and I knew it wasn't fair for me to blame it all on Alan. But I was Ollie's mother. I wasn't supposed to be the one corrupting him. I was the one who was supposed to be protecting him from the dangers of the world. I didn't think I could forgive myself if I ended up being responsible for turning Ollie into a Peeping Tom.

I sound so hypocritical, I thought. *The whole "do as I say, not as I do" line of crap isn't even flying with me. I'm just as guilty of invading those people's privacy as Alan and Ollie. I just hate admitting it.*

That morning, Alan was on the downstairs deck having a phone call with one of his partners at the firm. I was content to be up in our room. It was best we gave each other space until Ollie came home later that night.

I thought about what Alan had said the night before, about keeping photos and video recordings of the people we watch. I was curious which ones he had saved.

Alan's laptop was sitting on a small desk. I had never poked around on it. I never felt the need to, and I thought it wasn't right to do that. If I wanted to look at something on his laptop, all I would have to do was ask, and he would say it was fine. He would never tell me "no."

I opened it up, and a password field appeared. I knew Alan so well I was sure I could guess his password. He liked to read a Japanese comic called *Astro Boy,* so I punched in "Astroboy," and just like that, I had access.

I opened up his documents folder and looked around. Alan was the type to have every document on his laptop filed away properly in a folder. I found a folder labeled "The Residence."

Sheesh, Alan. It's a good thing you don't work for the CIA. You'd make a terrible spy.

I clicked on the folder and found more labeled folders. Some of the names I recognized, like the Mortons. The files were all video clips.

Why on Earth would he keep videos of those two?

I clicked on a video. The husband was sitting in front of the television, and his wife was in the kitchen, as usual. Suddenly she threw both arms up into the air and started yelling at him. He threw his arms up as if to say, "Here we go again." I actually remembered watching this one with Alan as it happened. It was funny then, and it was funny now. Was that why Alan kept it?

I opened a few other folders and watched the videos inside. It was all harmless. It was pretty dull stuff without the backstory we made up for context. I was about to shut his laptop when I spotted a folder titled "Blondie."

Hmmm.

I opened it, and it was filled with video files. I clicked on a video. It was the blonde woman Ollie had photographed.

He lied! I can't believe it.

She had just walked into her kitchen, fully clothed and drinking from a mug. I opened another one of her walking around her living room. I quickly opened more, searching for one where she was prancing around naked, but so far, they were all of her clothed. Still, I was pissed and shocked that Alan had lied.

Just then, I heard him coming up the stairs. I quickly closed the movie and the folders, then shut his laptop seconds before he appeared in our bedroom doorway.

"Hey, I just got a text from Ollie," he said. "They'll be home earlier than expected. I thought I'd fire up the grill later. How about ribeyes?"

"Oh, okay. Yeah, that sounds great."

He grabbed his wallet from the dresser. "You need anything from the store?"

"Not that I can think of."

"Okay, see you in a bit."

Yes, and you're getting an earful when you do.

Once I was sure Alan was out of the house, I opened his laptop again and navigated back to the "Blondie" folder. I searched the entire folder but found no sexy videos. Did he just not keep them, or was he having the same luck as Ollie? Was she simply some woman minding her own business in her apartment?

But what about her had spurred my husband and son to watch and document? Was this coincidental? Could Alan have told Ollie? Or worse, could Ollie have told Alan? But why? What was so special that one would need to tell the other? And what was the point of both of them documenting her? Was this some stupid guy thing that I would never ever be able to wrap my head around? I looked at the other folders and found one that surprised me. It was titled "Tiller."

Why would he be watching Tiller? We never watched him together.

I clicked on the folder, but it was empty. Did he have something in there and then delete it? Was he thinking of watching Tiller and setting up the folder in preparation?

One thing I knew about Mac laptops was that whatever is sent to the trash is recoverable unless you empty the trash. I clicked on the trash icon, and there were a bunch of documents with weird extensions I didn't want to mess with. I closed it and then opened up his email program. A quick scan told me it was all work-related stuff. Most of the emails were internal, and I recognized the names of his colleagues. I clicked on one with the subject line "The Proposal." It was someone responding to an email sent by Alan, pitching the firm's services.

I don't know why I continued to look at Alan's work email. What was I trying to gain? Did I think the woman worked at his firm? It would be weird if she did, since my husband and son were watching her. And then I saw a return email from Errol Tiller.

Why on Earth was Alan corresponding with Errol?

I clicked on it and saw that Errol was responding to an email Alan had sent him to confirm that his account with the firm had been canceled. All money under their management was to be returned. Tiller was inquiring why the account was closed and if he had done something wrong. His exact words: "I did everything you asked."

I didn't even know Alan had had Errol as a client—not that he had to tell me who their clients were. I didn't care. But I was slightly curious as to why they canceled his account. It appeared they were managing a couple of million dollars for him. I realized right then I was the one making everything strange. I was the one making up stories about every little thing.

You're losing it, Jill. You're becoming one of those conspiracy theory nuts. You're starting to see plots in everything you look at.

I suddenly felt guilty for snooping through Alan's laptop. How had I gone from worrying about the photo Ollie had taken to snooping through my husband's email?

Chapter Twenty-Three

Alan

I wish I were more of an outdoor guy and could have been the one who took Ollie and Grant camping over the weekend, but I was pretty clueless about that stuff. From what I understood, Grant's father, Kent, was one of those guys who grew up hunting, fishing, and camping. Ollie was in good hands.

I knew Jill and I needed to have this talk with Ollie as soon as he got home, which I wasn't looking forward to. But at the same time, I was excited he'd be home early. It meant he could come to the astronomy meetup later that night.

I hoped the talk would be quick and easy and not spoil our moods. But that would be up to Jill. She was the worried one. In my head, this was just horny teen stuff. Yeah, he shouldn't have been taking pictures, and I would tell him to stop and not do it again. But I didn't think we needed to give him the third degree. I was pretty sure he'd be embarrassed when we brought it up.

Was I hoping this wouldn't turn into a grilling? Sure. I had been watching people for as long as I could remember. I didn't think there was anything wrong with it. In fact, I thought watching could be a good thing. So how could I tell Ollie it was wrong when I was doing the same thing from my own bedroom? Well, I would say it starts with a couple of ground rules. For me, it wasn't sexual. It never had been and never would be. I was just fascinated by watching what I call "unedited humanity." Hopefully, that was the place it came from for Ollie, too.

When I returned home, I put the steaks in the fridge before heading upstairs.

"Jill," I called out as I headed into our bedroom. But Jill wasn't there.

I placed my wallet on the dresser and took a peek out on our balcony, but she wasn't there, either.

I headed down to Mia's room and knocked on her door. "Mia, sweetie. Can I come in?"

"Yeah, Dad."

I opened the door. "Have you seen your mother?"

"I think she went for a walk."

"A walk?"

"Yeah, I know. Go figure."

"What are you up to?"

"Just doing some homework. Why?"

"No reason. Just asking. Let me know if you need help, and I'll point you to the internet."

"Gee, thanks, Dad."

I shut Mia's door and headed into Ollie's room. In case Ollie knew something we didn't, we had left his camera functioning so that whatever it was could be captured. That was actually Jill's idea, not mine. But I didn't see any reason not to go along with it. I would want to know if he was up to something more than we were thinking. Either way, we would delete the pictures.

I peeked through the lens viewer and saw that the apartment was empty. I looked through Ollie's camera roll to see what had been captured since the last time we looked at it, and it was more of the same. Ollie's plan to document something interesting had turned out to be a bust.

Ollie could very well have had other photos on his computer. I didn't know the password, so he'd have to unlock it and let us have a look when he got back. I left Ollie's room, sticking to my own advice: innocent until proven guilty.

I headed back up to my bedroom and opened my laptop. I already knew the woman Ollie wanted to photograph. Well, I knew *of* her. I'd spotted her sometime around the beginning of summer. She caught my eye, and I watched, but there was nothing that interesting about her. Nonetheless, I did keep a couple of video captures, but only because I hadn't made up my mind about her.

Considering my son was also watching this woman, and we were about to ban him from doing it and tell him to delete everything, I needed to do the same. I deleted the folder I had named "Blondie," my nickname for her. I knew deleting the folder wasn't going to entirely solve my problems. I had other folders with captured footage from people we'd watched together. Why had I lied to Jill about it the other day? I guess the only answer was, I knew my wife. She had been in a space where saying the wrong thing would have sent her over the edge and possibly worsened things. So I lied—not to hide it from her forever, just to keep the situation stable until Ollie came home.

But Jill—if she was ever going to be okay with Ollie doing this, it would take time and effort to bring her around. I had a feeling she would shut it down. Period. No way she'd be okay with me telling Ollie it wasn't a problem. *Hey, guess what, Ollie? Your old man does the same thing. Welcome to the club, son.*

It would probably even affect our hobby. She might want to

stop watching, or even tell me to stop completely. Jill had always known who I was, and I believed she accepted it when she agreed to marry me. I loved her dearly, so if I needed to, I could stop for a while, for her. But could I stop forever? I wasn't sure of that.

Chapter Twenty-Four

Peggy Meyer

Ross and I were having our typical lazy Sunday together. It involved hanging out at our large kitchen island while eating breakfast and drinking coffee. That morning, I had made French toast, Ross's favorite. I had just finished the last sip of my coffee when the doorbell rang.

"Are you expecting someone?" my husband asked as he looked up from his phone.

"Nope. Sit, I'll get it."

At the bottom of the steps, I looked at myself in the wall mirror. I had my hair in a messy bun and wore a purple and yellow velour tracksuit. I looked cute and presentable for whoever might be visiting.

I peeked through a stained-glass window framing the front door and recognized the detectives from yesterday.

What the hell are they doing here?

"Detectives," I said with a smile as I opened the door. "What a surprise to find you on my doorstep."

"We apologize for bothering you at home on a Sunday morning," Detective Sokolov said.

"And yet you did."

"Nice house you have here," Detective Bennie said as he thumbed over his shoulder, "and a million-dollar view of the city to go with it."

"Thank you, but I'm sure you didn't come all this way to tell me that."

"We had some follow-up questions we'd like to ask," Detective Sokolov said.

He was the more serious of the two. All business and never cracked a smile. At the bottom of my driveway, I spied their navy blue Crown Victoria. They might as well have shown up in a black and white.

"And what questions might those be?"

"It's about your relationship with Mr. Tiller."

"I already told you this. Our relationship is professional. I interact with Errol on building issues, which isn't often. Sure, we say hello in the common areas, but I'm friendly with everyone in the building."

"We heard otherwise."

"And what did you hear? This ought to be good."

"We have a witness who saw you leave Mr. Tiller's apartment."

"So what? I've visited every apartment in the building. I'm the manager."

"This witness claims to have seen you kissing Mr. Tiller as you left his apartment."

I glanced over my shoulder before slipping out and closing the door. "Let's talk over there."

I led them to the bottom of the driveway, where the mailbox stood.

"Who is feeding you this absurd information?" I let out a tiny laugh as I lightly waved off the accusation.

Of course, several possible rats came to mind, but the one that stood out was Guy, our doorman. I'd always thought he was a nosy one. Was he gossiping with the detectives?

"Mrs. Meyer, were you in a relationship with Mr. Tiller?"

"A relationship? God, no."

I had a split second to decide if I should double down and continue denying or come clean. I had no idea what they knew. I could back myself into a corner if I kept denying the accusation. It was Guy's word against mine. He wasn't supposed to be on the upper floors—his domain was the lobby. But I didn't spend my days at work tracking people's movements.

"I'm sure this is all one big misunderstanding."

"Okay then, help us understand."

Detective Sokolov kept his gaze fastened on me. I could tell he wasn't backing down.

"Fine, I had a fling with Errol. So what? That's not a crime."

"No, it's not. But Mr. Tiller is dead."

"What? Do you think I killed him? Is this what this visit is really about?"

"All we're trying to do is find out what happened. You originally told us your relationship was professional. Now you've admitted that you had an intimate relationship with Mr. Tiller. You can understand how we might be thinking that there could be more information that you're withholding."

"And let me remind you," Detective Bennie said as he flashed his dimpled smile. "Impeding a police investigation is punishable with up to five years in prison, plus fines."

I can't believe this is my Sunday morning.

"How long were you seeing Mr. Tiller?" Detective Sokolov asked.

"Not that long, maybe six months. But I broke it off."

"When did this happen?" Detective Sokolov took out a pen and a small notepad.

"Earlier this week. I'd lost interest, and I know it doesn't look this way, but I love my husband. And no, he doesn't know anything about this, so I'd appreciate it if we kept this conversation private. Ross and I are happy. This thing with Errol, it was a huge mistake. He had his charming ways, and I allowed his advances to progress. I'm not proud of what I did."

"How did Mr. Tiller take the breakup?"

I shrugged. "Fine, I guess. If you're wondering if he broke down crying and begged me not to leave him, that didn't happen. Errol is rich and handsome. There is no shortage of women lining up to replace me."

"So your relationship was more than sex?"

"No, that's where I drew the line. I told Errol that I wasn't interested in anything more than a quickie every now and then after work."

"And he agreed?"

"He agreed. That was our relationship for six months."

"That's a long time to just have 'quickies,'" Detective Bennie said. "Sometimes relationships start off that way and progress. Maybe it progressed in Mr. Tiller's head."

"I don't think it did. I sort of got the feeling he might be screwing other women."

"And what makes you think that?"

"I saw a long strand of brown hair on his bathroom floor. As you can see, I'm a blonde."

"Did he ever mention seeing someone else?"

"No, that was Errol's charm. He was a master at making you feel special and important to him. I'm a strong-minded woman, and I usually don't fall for that stuff, but Errol had his ways."

"And since you broke it off, you haven't revisited Mr. Tiller's apartment?" Sokolov asked.

These bastards know. I can see it in their eyes. They want to catch me in another lie.

"Come to think of it, I did visit Errol's apartment on Friday night. I went to see him after I finished work."

"Do you mind telling us the reason for your visit?"

I let out a heavy breath. They were making me spell it out. "I had one last romp with him. But I swear that was the last time. He'd been begging me all week to do it one last time, and then we'd have a clean break."

"Why did you give in?"

"He threatened to tell my husband."

"Did you ever think he might continue to hold that threat over your head and force you to keep seeing him?" Detective Bennie asked. "Seems like he could, unless..."

"Unless what?"

"Unless you were able to do something about it."

"Of course, it crossed my mind. I told him I'd expose his cocaine use to his partners at his company and their clients."

I pulled my phone out and showed them a picture of Errol snorting cocaine. "I took this picture that night."

While looking at the photo of Errol, Detective Bennie took a picture of it with his phone and then asked her to forward it to him.

"Errol was on his way to another alcohol- and drug-infused night. Who knows what condition he was in when he went over that railing? His substance abuse was one of the reasons I wanted to break it off. I didn't want anything to do with that crap. I didn't partake. Look, detectives, I was there for thirty minutes, maybe forty-five. We had a drink, we screwed, and I left. My whole reason for going there was to take a photo like that. All I wanted was to put this thing with Errol behind me. But I assure you, he was alive when I left."

"Honey! Is everything okay?"

Ross had stuck his head out the front door.

"Everything's fine. I'll be back inside in a minute." I turned back toward the detectives. "Is there anything else?"

"You didn't happen to see Mr. Tiller's dog that last time you visited, did you?"

"Come to think of it, I didn't. But he wasn't one of those dogs that barked or greeted people at the front door. He preferred to lie off to the side, out of view. Why?"

"The dog's missing."

"I can't help you there, but you might want to talk to Geneva Garrett. She'd sometimes take Errol's dog out for a walk. She lives in the building with her mother. Stop by Monday afternoon, and I'll introduce you."

"We'll do that. We appreciate your cooperation, Mrs. Meyer."

I waited at the bottom of the driveway until the detectives drove away. On the walk back to the house, I thought more about the possible rat. Guy was pretty busy at his post all day long and he always left as soon as his shift was over. Ray spent most of the time in the basement like a hermit. That left Darrel as the little sniveling rat.

Ross was busy putting the dishes in the dishwasher when I returned.

"Who were those men?"

"That was Detective Sokolov and Detective Bennie of SFPD. They're investigating Errol Tiller's death." I took a seat next to the island.

"Investigating? I thought he committed suicide." Ross closed the dishwasher and turned it on.

"You and everyone else."

"They think he was murdered?"

"I don't know what they're thinking, but they had a few more questions."

A frown appeared on his face as he leaned against the

island. "Couldn't they have waited until Monday? What kind of pressing questions could they have had for you?"

"I had the same thought. They wanted to know if I knew anyone in the building who didn't get along with Errol."

"Are there people like that?"

"Not that I'm aware of."

"What else did they ask?"

"What do you mean, 'what else'?"

"You were talking to them for a while."

"Like I said, it was just a bunch of mundane questions. I wish they met with me on Monday instead of disturbing us." I draped my arms around his neck and snuggled into his chest, breathing in his scent. "This is our time, and you know I hate it when work interferes with our time."

I think I'll fire Darrel on Monday morning. I can't have him running his mouth like that.

Chapter Twenty-Five

Ollie

A STORM WAS EXPECTED to hit Sierra on Sunday evening, so Grant's father wanted to leave earlier than we had planned. It wasn't that big of a deal; we were leaving the campsite at two instead of five.

Grant and I slept for most of the drive back. I woke when Mr. Walker pulled into our driveway. I thanked him and said goodbye to Grant before grabbing my things and heading inside.

I headed straight upstairs to my bedroom and dropped my stuff on the floor. I hurried over to the camera, eager to see what I had captured over the weekend. Instead, I found a sticky note with the message: *We need to talk —Mom & Dad.*

Shit!

I heard a throat being cleared, and I spun around. Standing in the doorway were my parents. My mom had her arms folded across her chest. That was never a good thing.

"Hi, Ollie," my mom said. "Did you have a nice time?"

"Uh, yeah. We caught a lot of fish."

My parents came inside, and my dad shut the door behind him.

"I think you can guess what we need to talk about," my mom

said. "Explain to your father and me what you were doing with your camera?"

I looked away from them, focusing on my bed. "This is so embarrassing. I can't."

"I don't care. Start talking."

"Well, I was taking pictures..."

"Speak up," my dad said. "And elaborate."

"I said I was taking pictures...of an apartment in the building Grant lives in."

"Why?" my mom asked.

"I don't know."

"Ollie," she prodded, raising her voice.

"I was trying to photograph the person who lives there."

"And who lives there?" my dad asked.

I didn't know what to say.

"We're just having a conversation here," he said. "You're not in trouble."

"She's a teacher from my school."

"A teacher!" My mom exploded. "Ollie, why are you spying on a teacher from school?"

"Jill, let him explain."

"I'm sorry. I know it's wrong, and I shouldn't be doing it."

"Ollie, take a seat," my dad said. "We're not here to crucify you. Your mother and I are just concerned, that's all."

I sat on the edge of my bed.

"I know how bad it looks," I said.

"You're right, it looks pretty bad. So why did you do it?" my mom asked.

"It wasn't even my idea. It was Grant's."

"Why would Grant want you to photograph your teacher all weekend?" my mom asked.

"Because she's hot, and I knew I could if I used Dad's intervalometer."

"What's this teacher's name?"

"It's Ms. Martin. She's, like, a substitute teacher."

My dad sat beside me and put his arm around my shoulder. "Ollie, there's nothing wrong with admiring a beautiful woman, but taking pictures of her inside her apartment every few minutes is a little overboard. Were you trying to catch something in particular?"

"Not really. At the time, we were just excited that we could see her. Grant found out she lived in his building a few months ago, and when he finally figured out which floor she lived on, we started searching for her apartment. Well, he told me, and I started searching."

"And then?"

"I told him I found it, and he asked me to take some pictures, so I did."

My mom sighed. "Ollie, tell me you didn't send these photos to Grant."

"I did, but he said he would delete them, and I told him not to pass them around because I didn't want to get into trouble if anyone found out I took them."

"How do you know Grant won't do that anyway?" my mom asked.

I shrugged. "I don't know. Because it's Grant, and he's my best friend."

"Ollie, besides the photos on your camera roll, did you download other photographs?" my dad asked.

I nodded. "There's a folder on my laptop."

"Open it. Show us," my mom said.

I couldn't believe I was about to show my mom nude pictures of Ms. Martin, but I went ahead and navigated to the folder where I kept all the photos.

"This is it. I promise."

"Are there nude photos of her in that collection?" my mom

asked.

"Yes," I said softly.

"Delete them all now. Same with the ones on your camera."

"Ollie, is it just you and Grant who know about these photos?" my dad asked.

"Yeah. I know Grant hasn't shared them with anyone. We're not stupid... Are you telling Ms. Martin what I did?"

"No, but I want you to promise your mother and me that you won't take more pictures of her."

"I won't. I promise."

"And that goes for anyone else. Is she the only one?" my mom asked.

"Yeah."

"I also want you to double-check and make sure Grant hasn't made copies. If he did, I want them deleted. Is that clear?"

"I promise, I'll make sure he doesn't have any."

My mom left my bedroom without saying anything more. My dad detached his intervalometer from my camera.

"Astronomy only. Got it?" he said.

"Yeah, Dad."

"Hey, since you're home early, want to go to the astronomy meetup with me tonight?"

"Yeah, that'll be great. But uh, Dad...aren't you and mom grounding me?"

"I don't think so. But your mother isn't happy about this, and I'm not either. We'll leave at seven, okay?"

"Okay."

Chapter Twenty-Six

Jill

I WAS out on the deck when Alan came up behind me. He wrapped his arms around my stomach and hugged me gently.

"You okay with how that talk went?"

"I guess. We kind of already knew what the reason was, but the teacher reveal surprised us."

"Do you know her?" he asked.

I was involved with many of the school's functions, so I'd gotten to know Ollie's teachers.

"I don't, but he said she's a substitute. That could be why."

"That's a good thing, right? It means once her contract is over, she's gone."

"She might be gone from the school, but she'll still live in the Middle Finger."

"True."

"You think Ollie will continue to watch her?"

"Honestly? Probably. But I think it'll pass. Something else will catch his interest."

"Some*thing* else, or some*one* else?"

"Could be both, I guess."

"How can you be so relaxed about this?"

"I don't see the point in getting worked up."

"Are you saying I'm overreacting?"

"I'm saying I don't want it to get that way. It has nothing to do with you. It's not like Ollie is out robbing homes. He's watching people. You know I've always thought it could be a good thing."

"I know."

"After you left, Ollie asked if we were grounding him."

"What did you tell him?"

"I told him you and I needed to discuss it."

I looked up at Alan. "Do you think he should be grounded?"

"I think he just experienced the most embarrassing moment with us to date. I think that's punishment enough. Do you want to ground him?"

"I don't know. I want to see how I feel after a few hours. If anything, taking away his camera equipment would be a better punishment."

"What about the school's photography club? Isn't Ollie the one who heads it up?"

"That's right. He'll need it for that. What if we told him he could only use it at the club?"

"Jill, I don't think they really use the cameras at the club meeting. I think they use it outside, and when they meet, they share what photographs they took."

"Oh. Well, help me think of something."

"Why do we need to punish him? I'm not sure what more that will gain us."

"We need to punish him so he learns."

"He realizes he messed up. We need to trust that Ollie's responsible enough not to do it again."

"And if he does?"

"Cameras are gone. Plain and simple. I'm going to fire up the grill and prepare the steaks."

Alan kissed the top of my head and turned to go back inside. It made me feel better. I wasn't really angry with Ollie. I was still caught up in my own hypocrisy. Guilty was more like what I felt.

I had brought a telescope to the balcony, and I fixed it on the Middle Finger, just to take a peek and see if Ms. Martin was home. To my surprise, she was. I jumped back from the telescope, feeling like she could see me, which was ridiculous. I looked through the eyepiece again. She had disappeared.

Wait, did I imagine that?

I double-checked, counting the floors from the top down to make sure I had the right apartment. I did—plus, I recognized the furniture. Then she reappeared, stepping out from her bedroom. This time, she was dressed in a skimpy bikini. She stood in front of the glass doors leading to her balcony and started snapping selfies. I guess the light was good there. *I definitely have not seen this woman at a school function.* She then switched on some portable lights.

After taking a dozen or so selfies, she stopped, took off her bikini top, and proceeded to take a bunch more selfies.

Let me guess, after this, you're stripping off your bottoms and taking more photos.

Sure enough, she did exactly that.

She must know people can see her standing there... Actually, they would only be able to see her if they had a telescope or binoculars and knew to look there. You know, just like what you're doing.

Well, at least the photos would be tasteful. I had to give her that.

Whoops, spoke too soon. That's an interesting pose. Maybe she's got a boyfriend, and it's his birthday, or perhaps she...is that a toy? Yup, that's a toy. Okay, I'm done.

I pulled away just as I heard Mia come up behind me.

"Mom, whatcha looking at?" she asked as she leaned against the balcony railing.

"Uh, nothing." I nonchalantly swiveled the telescope a few degrees north. "What's up?"

"I need a book for class. Can you order it for me online?"

"Yeah, just write down the name for me."

"I have it right here." She handed me a piece of paper. "Thanks."

I stopped Mia just as she turned. "What class is this for?"

"History, why?"

"Just asking. How's history?"

"It's fine."

"And school in general...everything okay?"

"Yeah. Why all the questions?"

"I have a meeting tomorrow with some of the other mothers. I want to make sure I'm up to scratch on all things school related."

"Uh, okay."

"Any new teachers I should know about?"

Mia shrugged. "Oh, there is this one teacher the boys all have a crush on, Ms. Martin. But she's only a substitute. I don't even know if she's still there. I haven't seen her lately."

"Ah, okay. I'll get the book for you," I said as Mia left.

I'll admit, I was relieved to hear that it wasn't just Ollie, it was all the boys lusting over Ms. Martin. Maybe Alan was right. Maybe it was just a passing teenage boy thing.

Chapter Twenty-Seven

Ollie

I PROBABLY SPENT a solid ten minutes by myself in silence, contemplating the humiliation of admitting to my mom that I had taken naked photos of my teacher. I couldn't even look her in the eyes. At least my dad tried to be cool about it. He probably thought it was no big deal. But my mom—it'll be awkward with her for years, even when I'm grown and come to visit for Thanksgiving. I picked up my cell and video-called Grant.

"Yo, what's up?" he said. "Did you get some good pictures? Tell me you got some of her changing."

"Dude, you'll never believe what just went down."

"What?"

"My mom found out about my camera taking photos of Ms. Martin's apartment."

"No way. How did she find out?"

"I left my bedroom door open when I left to go camping."

"Damn, dude. So what happened?"

"I had to delete all the photos."

"Really? That blows. Did you at least get a chance to go through them?"

"Nope. She and my dad were totally waiting for me when I

got home. Not only did I have to delete those, I also had to get rid of all the others I had taken from before. Dude, it was horrible. I had to admit to my mom that I was taking naked pictures of my teacher."

Grant started to laugh uncontrollably.

"Don't laugh, dude. You need to delete all the photos I sent you. My mom will go over there and tell your mom if she doesn't believe you deleted them."

"Are you serious?"

"Dead serious. Trust me. She won't give a shit if your parents find out and ground you until you're thirty. Promise me you'll delete any pictures you have of Ms. Martin."

"Okay, okay. Which ones are you talking about? The nude ones or the sex ones?"

"All of them! You don't need them anymore. I'm deleting them, too. By the way, did your mom say anything to you about Mr. Tiller?"

"No, and I don't think she will, but there already seems to be less tension. I mean, I'm still a little pissed at her, but not like before."

"That's good."

"Yeah, that guy really screwed things up. I'm so glad he's gone."

"Yeah, man, you'll never have to worry about Mr. Tiller again."

"Hey, I gotta go. Talk to you later."

"Later."

I disconnected the video call and spun around in my desk chair, only to find my mom standing in the doorway with her arms crossed over her chest. Again.

"What do you mean 'you'll never have to worry about Mr. Tiller again'?" she asked.

"It's nothing, mom."

"It sure doesn't sound like nothing. I'll ask one more time. What did you mean when you said 'you don't need to worry about Mr. Tiller again'?"

I stared at the carpet, once again unable to look my mom in the eyes.

"Because of what Mr. Tiller did."

"What did he do?"

"Grant's mom was cheating with Mr. Tiller."

My mom raised her eyebrows. "How do you know that?"

"Because I saw her on Mr. Tiller's balcony kissing him. I took a picture and showed it to Grant."

"Are you sure?"

"Mom, I know what Mrs. Walker looks like."

"What happened when you told Grant?"

"He freaked out."

"I can imagine. Does Mr. Walker know about this?"

"No, he doesn't, mom. And you can't tell him. The only people who know are Grant and me and now you."

"So this is why you were taking photos of Ms. Martin?"

"Sort of...not really. After Grant found out about his mom cheating, he confronted her."

"He did? What happened?"

"She denied it until he showed her the picture. That's when she admitted what she did, and she said she was sorry. She said she would end it and not to tell his dad."

"So, did she end it?"

"As far as we know. But we have no proof."

"So how does Ms. Martin fit into all of this?"

I shrugged. "What I told you earlier was the truth. We just think she's hot."

"Something tells me the story doesn't end here."

"Mom, you have to believe me when I tell you I had no idea he would do this with the photo."

"Do what, Ollie?"

"Promise me, Mom."

"Okay, I promise."

I took a moment to figure out the best way to tell her.

"Grant sent Mr. Tiller the photo I took of him making out with Mrs. Walker and told him he would beat the crap out of him if he didn't stop."

"He did *what*?"

"But he made up a fake email account so Mr. Tiller wouldn't know Grant sent the email. It was just to scare him."

"Threatening the man with violence. Do you think that's okay? You realize that's illegal, right?"

"Mom, I didn't know Grant planned to do this. Remember, you promised to believe me."

"Ollie, Mr. Tiller is dead! Do you realize how this looks? I can't believe this."

My mom stormed out of my room and yelled at the top of her lungs. "Alan! Could you come up here?"

"What's going on?" Mia asked as she came running into my bedroom.

"A shit show." I rolled my eyes.

A few seconds later, my mom reappeared, dragging my father by his arm. He had his grilling apron on.

"Alan, I want you to listen. Ollie, start over."

"From what part?"

"From when you told Grant he doesn't have to worry about Mr. Tiller anymore."

Chapter Twenty-Eight

Kelly Walker

I'D BEEN WAITING all day for Kent and Grant to return from their camping trip. I had thought the time to myself would be great, but it wasn't. I felt lonely and missed my family. Sure, I wanted Kent to have his father-son bonding time, but that wasn't why Kent had suggested the trip in the first place. He thought Grant was in a teenage funk and getting away for a few days might breathe life back into him.

A funk wasn't the problem. The cold shoulder, ignoring my presence, pretending not to hear me—it wasn't Grant being a teenager. It was because of what I had done.

I thought time would make things better, but it didn't. Grant seemed to be pulling further and further away. I don't think he and I spoke more than a few words during the weeks leading up to the camping trip. I didn't blame him for turning against me. I was the one who broke his trust.

I still remember the day he confronted me. It was seared into my memory. I was in the kitchen when he'd come home from school. He threw his backpack onto the floor and stared at me. I asked him what was wrong and if anything had happened at school that day. He ignored me at first, but after I kept pressing him, he snapped.

"Damn, Mom! How could you?"

Grant had never raised his voice at me, ever. I was utterly shocked and remember thinking, "This can't be my child." As I struggled to respond, he pulled out his cell phone and showed me the picture, the one of me kissing Errol on his balcony.

It felt like I had died a thousand deaths. My knees felt weak, and the room began to spin. I had to use the counter to steady myself. Do you know how it feels to have your child confront you about your infidelity? Pray that you never find out. There are no words to describe the immense shame I felt at that moment. I could barely manage to look my son in the eye. And when I did, all I saw was a hurt little boy—my boy. Tears ran down the sides of his red cheeks as he drew sharp, choppy breaths. I reached out to try and comfort him, and he swatted at my hand.

"I can't believe you cheated on Dad," he said.

I had no answer other than to say, "I'm sorry."

"You're sorry? Really? Or are you just sorry you got caught?"

Sadly, it was the latter. But I also realized at that moment that my actions had real consequences. I couldn't explain to Grant why I did what I did. All I could do was tell him that I did love his father very much and that I was wrong. I had made a grave mistake.

I badly wanted to console Grant, but all he wanted was to be anywhere but near me.

From that day on, our relationship changed. I was invisible to Grant. Of course, Kent picked up on it pretty quickly. I played along, brainstorming with my husband on a problem I already knew the answer to—a problem of my own making.

There I was, suggesting fake reasons for Grant's behavior. I even suggested he go to therapy.

But I couldn't tell Kent the real reason. I didn't want to lose him. Yes, I cheated. Yes, it was stupid. But it didn't mean my family wasn't important to me. I loved Kent and Grant very much, and if I could go back in time and change things, I would. Every day, I would walk around the apartment on eggshells, wondering if today was the day Grant would show his father the photo.

I had broken it off with Errol earlier the same day Grant confronted me. I told him that, but it made no difference. The damage had been done. I sensed that my son no longer believed anything I said. No surprises there. All I could do was hope that, over time, I could earn his trust back. I know what I did was extremely selfish. And so was pretending every day that nothing had happened. I even stopped showing my husband affection in front of Grant. I hated that he judged me.

Every once in a while, I would catch Grant looking at me, his gaze burning into my skin like hot daggers. I had approached him numerous times to try and smooth things out between us, but he rejected me each time. As time passed, Grant's attitude became a bigger issue for Kent. He even told Grant that he didn't appreciate his attitude and it had to stop. I knew it was only a matter of time before Grant told Kent, and that would be the end of our family.

But then Kent suggested the camping trip, and for the first time in weeks, Grant exhibited signs of happiness.

I had just received a text from Kent telling me they would be home in ten minutes. To say I was nervous was an understatement. When they walked through that door, I knew I would have an answer: Would I continue with my pretending, or would there finally be a breakthrough with Grant? I took a seat on the sofa and waited.

A few moments later, I heard footsteps in the hall come to a stop, the jingle of keys, and then the door unlocking. I drew a breath and stood.

"Hi, Mom," Grant said as he threw his arms around me and hugged me. "It's good to be home. But, man, I gotta drop the kids off at the pool if you know what I mean."

He left his gear on the floor and hurried to the bathroom. I turned to my husband as he wrapped his arms around me for a hug.

"He's back to normal. I told you the trip would—"

I dropped to the floor, heaving and sobbing uncontrollably as relief washed over me. I couldn't believe it. My son, my little boy... I had gotten the answer I desperately wanted.

Chapter Twenty-Nine

Jill

OLLIE HAD WALKED Alan through everything he had relayed to me. And when he missed a detail, I either prompted or filled it in for him.

Alan ran a hand through his hair as he shook his head. "I'm at a loss for words."

"But Dad, you have to understand. I didn't know Grant would send the photo to Mr. Tiller and threaten him."

"I know, but he did, and it's done. It just doesn't look very good."

"It looks terrible, Alan."

"Hold on, Jill. There's nothing criminal about photographing two people on a balcony."

"But he threatened Errol with violence."

"Let's be clear here. Grant threatened Errol with violence. Not Ollie."

I turned to my son. "Are you telling us the truth about not knowing anything about what Grant had planned?"

"I swear, Mom. I'm telling the truth. I was shocked when Grant told me, but at the same time, I knew he was angry about what had happened. It messed with his head."

"I can't believe Mrs. Walker cheated," Mia said. "How did her husband not find out? I mean, they're in the same building."

Ollie shrugged. "I don't know. I never really asked questions. I only listened to Grant when he needed to vent."

"Alan, should we talk to the Walkers? I think we need to get this out in the open."

"You can't do that, mom. Grant's dad doesn't know."

"Ollie's right. That's a private issue for their family to deal with. As for the threat—I don't think Grant had anything to do with Errol's death."

"Geez, Dad, you think Grant killed Mr. Tiller?"

"I just said I don't think so. I'm trying to think of what the police might be thinking. Right now, they're investigating the cause of his death. There's a chance they might poke around in his email and find the one Grant sent."

"And that's exactly why I'm wondering if we should at least talk to Kelly," I said.

"Jill, Ollie didn't send the email. He took the picture, and so what? I say we wait and see how this plays out for now."

"God, Ollie, you need to stop taking pictures of people," Mia said. "Who else are you taking pictures of? I hope people at school don't find out. I might—"

"Mia, that's enough," I said. "Not a word of what we discussed here to anyone. Is that understood?"

"Fine."

"Ollie, is there anything else you need to tell us?" I asked. "Because now would be the time to get it out."

Ollie broke eye contact with me, and I knew the answer right then and there.

"Ollie?"

"Ollie, just spit it out already," Mia said.

"Shut up!" he shot back at his sister.

"Mia, not another word from you," I said. "In fact, go to your room."

"Why? I think I should hear what Ollie has to say. I'm just as much a part of this family as Ollie, and this will affect me, too."

I sighed. "Just keep your comments to yourself unless we ask for your opinion."

"Come on, Ollie. What else is there?" Alan asked.

"Okay, I want to repeat what I said before. If I tell you something, you have to promise not to get mad at—"

"Ollie," Alan said with a raised voice. "Do *not* make us repeat ourselves."

Very rarely was Alan the one to raise his voice at the kids. It felt good for the roles to be reversed for once. Ollie looked as if he had shrunk a foot and a half.

"Okay, okay," he said. "There are other pictures I didn't tell you about." He glanced at Mia.

"Never mind your sister," I said. "Continue."

"We have pictures of Mr. Tiller having sex with Ms. Martin."

"You what?"

Please tell me I didn't hear what I thought I heard.

"We have pictures," he said quietly.

I never thought I would become my mother, but there I was, weight shifted to one foot, hand resting on my hip with what surely had to be a look of disappointment. All I needed to do was look up and cry, "What in God's name will I do with you?" I finally understood how a child could drive a parent to the edge. There I stood, teetering.

I might as well stick my chin out and tell Ollie to sock me a good one. It would be less painful than hearing the excuse my son had waiting in the wings.

Ollie cleared his throat. "Because we were watching Ms.

Martin, we—well, I—accidentally stumbled across them. I wasn't trying to. I didn't even know Mr. Tiller knew Ms. Martin. But one day, I looked into her apartment and saw Mr. Tiller. He and Ms. Martin were playing around with those masks that people wear at Mardi Gras. I thought it was funny, so I took photos. I planned to send them to Grant for a good laugh."

"Wait, was this before or after you found out Grant had sent Mr. Tiller the other photo with the threat?" Alan asked.

"This was before."

"Okay, continue."

"They disappeared from view, but when they returned, Mr. Tiller was dressed in a schoolboy costume. Ms. Martin was dressed like a teacher, or maybe a librarian—not like a real teacher, but a costume. She was even holding a ruler, but they were both wearing masks at that point. That's when they started pretending, like doing a skit, and the next thing I know, they were stripping off their clothes and getting into it. But the weird thing is, she had a camera set up. She was filming."

"You mean the camera was out in the open? Like Errol knew what she was doing?" I asked.

"Yeah. He even looked through the viewfinder."

"Oh, my God," Mia said. "I bet Ms. Martin has an OF account. Why else would she be filming it?"

"What's an OF account?" I asked.

"OF is short for OnlyFans," Mia said. "People can post pictures and videos on their page and charge other people money to look at them. It's totally a legit side hustle—not that I would do it, because I have you and Dad—but I'm just saying, you know, if I were short of cash, it's a viable option. But again, I don't have to, because I have you and Dad."

Still teetering.

"So you have these photos of them, and you sent it to Grant for laughs?" Alan asked.

"Yeah, plus it's Ms. Martin."

"Ollie, do you still have these photos?" I asked.

"Yes, but I was about to delete them. And I told Grant to do the same, but that's when you came into my room."

"Ollie, did Grant do anything with those photographs?" Alan asked.

"I swear he only told me after he did it. I had no idea he planned this."

"He sent them to Errol, didn't he?"

"Yeah. That's when he finally told me what he did with the picture of Mr. Tiller with his mom. Grant said he never got a response, so when I sent him these photos, he emailed them to Mr. Tiller, threatening to post them online if he didn't leave his mom alone."

"What happened?" I asked.

"I don't know. Grant only told me what he did last week. And then the next thing we knew, Mr. Tiller was dead."

I looked over at Alan. "What are we going to do?"

Chapter Thirty

Kelly

I EVENTUALLY PULLED myself together after Kent lifted me off the floor. He hugged me for what seemed like an eternity. And I hugged him back. I was so happy. It was the start of our family getting back to normal. And the only person who could theoretically screw it up was dead.

I won't lie, I was relieved when I first heard the news about Errol. I no longer had the threat of exposure from him looming over my head. When I broke it off with Errol, I thought I'd never hear from him again. Wrong. Later that evening, he sent me a text message saying he wasn't finished with me. At first, I ignored his messages, but then the frequency increased. He finally said if I didn't come over for an afternoon visit, he would tell my husband about us.

I couldn't believe it. If my son didn't tell Kent, Errol would. What were the odds? I thought of coming clean to Kent just so he would hear it from me. I was prepared to accept my fate, even if it meant Kent filing for divorce. But then he mentioned the camping trip, and something inside me told me to wait and see what came from it. Maybe it would make a difference with Grant. And if it could, I certainly didn't want to derail it.

And then news of Errol's death came. Errol was out of the picture, and all I had to do was focus on my son. There was finally a sliver of light at the end of the tunnel.

"What happened up there? Did you two talk?" I asked Kent.

"We fished, hiked, roasted marshmallows...typical camping stuff. I never brought up the subject, and neither did Grant. In fact, he spent a lot of time with Ollie. I just knew everyone was having a fun, relaxing time. I think that's what Grant needed: time away from the city."

"It's like night and day. It's been so long since I hugged him."

Kent wiped a tear off my cheek. "Probably best not to let him see you like this."

I grabbed a tissue and dried my face. "I'm just glad my son is back."

"Me too."

I heard the toilet flush, and a few moments later, Grant appeared. "Hey, I was thinking, it's been a long time since we watched a horror movie together. We should do that tonight. Mom, remember how scared you always get?"

I laughed. "Yes, I remember."

"Sounds like a great idea, Grant," Kent said.

"Cool. I'm going to shower. I smell like fish."

After Grant left the room, I turned to my husband. "I love you. Thank you for doing all of this."

"I love you, too, honey. I'd do anything to see that smile back on your face."

I grabbed another tissue and blew my nose. "Maybe we should order a pizza for later," I said.

"Yup, good idea. Hey, did you hear about Errol? Terrible thing to have happened."

"Yes, I did. The police and the media were here all morning."

"Did they ever come to a conclusion as to what happened?"

"I'm not sure, but everyone says it was suicide."

"Wow, sometimes you never know, huh?"

"What do you mean?"

"Whenever I'd pass him in the lobby, he seemed happy. I guess some people are good at hiding their demons."

"I guess so."

Chapter Thirty-One

Jill

DINNER WAS AWKWARD. And I don't think anyone enjoyed the steak Alan had grilled, except for him. Nothing could dim his appetite in all the years I'd known him. I did my best to make conversation normal by asking the kids questions about school, but after a litany of "yes," "no," and "I dunno," I gave in and let the clanking of cutlery against plates carry on uninterrupted.

As soon as Mia finished her food, she excused herself and went to her room. Ollie followed minutes later, leaving Alan and me alone at the dinner table. We had decided to table the Ollie situation until after dinner.

"Have you been thinking about it?" I asked him.

"I have. And as angry as I am that he withheld that information, I don't think we have anything to worry about. I know you're thinking it doesn't look good, considering the timing of Errol's death, but it's not like either one of them pushed Errol off his balcony. They were camping."

"You're right, but what if it's implied that the email drove Errol to throw himself over the balcony? Like he really believed the threat? I'm talking about the one with him making the porn video. I mean, that could possibly drive him to suicide, right?"

"You have a point. Here's what I'll do. One of my clients is a criminal defense lawyer here in town. Let me bounce this situation off him and see what he thinks."

"You want to hire a lawyer?"

"Not hire, consult. I'm sure he'll tell us if we need to hire him. My real concern is Grant. He's not our child, so we can't control him. At least with Ollie, we know he deleted the photos. So there's no chance they can be used again."

"I still think we should talk to Kelly Walker."

"Let's see what the lawyer says about Ollie tomorrow and what he advises us to do."

Alan stood and started clearing the table.

"Are you still heading to your astronomy meeting tonight?" I asked as I helped him.

"Yeah, I don't see any need to miss it."

"Are you taking Ollie?"

"Yeah, why?"

"Just asking. I mean, it seems like embarrassment is the only punishment. He lied to us twice. I know he thinks he's just protecting his friend."

"I want to paint the basement. What if I make him help me? Or better yet, make him paint it himself?"

"Seems like just a guy thing," I said as I followed Alan into the kitchen.

He started rinsing off the dishes and putting them into the dishwasher. "Okay, what if it was a teaching punishment? He needs to help out at the soup kitchen once a week for a month. How does that sound? And on top of it, he has to take pictures and put on a show at school, encouraging others to volunteer."

"Hmmm, that sounds okay with me."

"Good, then it's settled. I'll tell him on our way back from the meeting." Alan dried his hands on a dish towel. "Anything else you want to say?"

"Yes. When were you planning on telling me you knew about Ms. Martin?"

Alan crossed his arms and leaned back against the counter. "I figured you'd find out. I discovered her about two months ago." He shrugged. "The only reason I didn't share her with you is that, to be honest, she was kind of boring. Nothing like the Mortons. And no, I'm not bothered by the fact that you snooped around my laptop. I've got nothing to hide from you, you know that. How did you guess my password?"

"You're predictable, Astro Boy. Why did you keep a video of her if she was so boring?"

Alan shrugged. "It's one of those things where, if I deleted it, I'd think of a reason why I needed it the next day. But I deleted the video today. It's gone."

He must have seen from my expression that I wasn't totally satisfied, because he kept talking. "And there were no nudes. I actually never saw what Ollie saw."

"I know there were no nudes. Alan, why did you have Errol as a client?"

"Because he approached the firm about a year ago wanting us to manage some funds for him. He said you recommended me."

"He did? I don't recall telling him you could manage his money."

"Maybe you just mentioned my line of work."

"Could be. Why did you stop doing business with him?"

"Because he's a small account, to begin with, and over time he started withdrawing funds. That's usually a sign someone is having financial problems. I tried to talk to him, but he refused. So the firm made the decision to cut him loose. He was more of a hassle than a source of revenue."

"I can't believe I'm discovering all these connections this

family has to Errol—you handling his funds, and Ollie and the pictures."

"Yeah, it's strange. All we need is Mia to reveal a skeleton, and that'll be everyone except for you." Alan winked at me.

"Don't say that. You'll jinx it. And anyway, she already has a connection. The internship."

"That's right. You know, I'm proud of us. All things considered, we seem to be handling this calmly."

"We are, aren't we?"

"I'm going to clean the grill. Care to help?"

"Nah, I know how much you enjoy it. Knock yourself out."

I headed back upstairs, thinking how glad I was that one of us thought everything was kosher. But I knew better than to relax like Alan. Errol was dead. And I had watched enough true crime television to know that if the police established a motive, they were well on their way to making an arrest.

As I hit the landing on the second floor, I saw that Mia and Ollie had their doors closed. A visual of Ollie looking at Ms. Martin's apartment popped into my head. Was he peeping on her right now? I continued up the stairs but stopped halfway and quietly headed back to Ollie's room. The floors were carpeted, so sneaking up to his door was easy. I carefully placed my ear next to his door and listened. I heard nothing. Was that a good thing or a bad thing? Shouldn't he be getting ready for the astronomy meetup? I wasn't sure exactly what that entailed. Maybe he was listening to music through his headset.

I stepped away from his door and went up to my bedroom. The following morning, I had a meeting scheduled with the other moms involved in planning the fall social at the school. I wondered what any of them knew about the substitute teacher. Mia made it seem like Ms. Martin was popular at school, at least with the boys. Someone had to know something.

Chapter Thirty-Two

Helen

I NEVER THOUGHT I'd give up paddling men in New York for a career making scented candles in San Francisco. But there I was, a candle queen with a growing business.

My alarm went off at seven, and I crawled out of bed. I slept in the nude and liked to stay that way until I had at least two cups of coffee inside me. I pulled open the drapes, letting the sunlight fill my apartment. *Hello, Monday.*

I had an unobstructed view of San Francisco Bay. To my right was the Bay Bridge. To my left was Alcatraz Island. And farther back, the Golden Gate Bridge. I stood there, in front of my floor-to-ceiling windows, admiring the view for a few moments. I was so glad I had made the leap to move to San Francisco. My only regret was Errol Tiller—that rat bastard.

I'd wake with a smile and then remember my connection with him. I was so stupid to send those emails. I kept waiting for that knock on my door by the police.

I was reading the *New York Daily News* and working on my first cup of coffee when a knock on my front door caught my attention. I glanced at my phone.

Who's visiting me at 8:30?

I thought the police wouldn't visit that early in the morning unless it was SWAT, so that quelled my fear. But now I was annoyed. I quickly put on a robe and looked through the peephole. Standing outside was Peggy Meyer, the building manager.

What the hell does she want?

I cracked the door open enough to look at her.

"Peggy?"

"Hello, Helen. So sorry to bother you this early in the morning, but you have some guests." It was only then that I noticed the two men in suits.

"This is Detective Sokolov and Detective Bennie with the San Francisco Police. They needed to ask you some questions," she said. "I'll leave you be."

And just like that, she turned and left.

"We apologize for the early visit," Detective Sokolov said. "We'll try and make this as quick as possible."

I pulled the door all the way open and motioned for them to come inside.

"Do you guys want coffee? I have a fresh pot."

They looked at each other before nodding their heads. I told them to sit on the couch while I went and poured coffee into two mugs.

"Do you need cream or sugar?" I asked from the kitchen.

"No, we're good with it black."

"Good, because that's the only way I drink it. So, what sort of questions do you have?"

I handed them each a mug before sitting on a chair opposite them.

"Nice place you have here," Detective Bennie said. "The view of the bay is incredible."

"I'm glad I'm on this side and not facing Nob Hill. I have a friend who lives on the hill. She hates this building because it spoils her view."

"Could you tell us what kind of relationship you had with Mr. Tiller?" Detective Sokolov asked.

"What makes you think I even knew the guy? Aside from waving in the lobby, I didn't know him."

Detective Bennie removed a piece of paper from an envelope and placed it on the coffee table.

"This is Mr. Tiller's phone record. These are the phone numbers he called and texted, and the people who called and texted him. The highlighted number is yours. As you can see, you two have been in contact with each other. Please elaborate on your relationship with Mr. Tiller."

A couple of thoughts raced through my head right then. They clearly had the phone records. But did they have the emails? What about bank transfers? How much did they know, and how many lies could I be caught in before they arrested me?

Detective Sokolov took a sip from his mug. "Good coffee."

I stood up and adjusted my robe. "Gentlemen, please follow me."

I led them down the hallway and into my master bedroom. I had a fantastic walk-in closet, which Errol had had custom built when I moved into the place.

"Come on. Don't be shy. I'm not."

My walk-in closet was lined with clothing on both sides. The wall at the rear was where I kept my shoes, and down the middle was a storage island. I stopped and pulled open a drawer, revealing a collection of leather clothing.

"Take a look. These are the outfits I wore when I worked as a dominatrix back in New York. I was semi-retired here in San Francisco, with one customer: Errol. I guess you could say I'm fully retired now."

"So that's the nature of the communication between you two?" Detective Sokolov asked.

"That's right. But there's no longer a need for me to protect my client's privacy. I'm sorry I wasn't forthcoming with you from the start. Old habits die hard."

"Does this mean you frequented Mr. Tiller's apartment?"

"Yes, we would hold sessions in his apartment. On occasion, we would hold them at a local BDSM club. They have equipment there that I don't own. Sometimes Errol would want to go there. He liked the dungeon aspect of it."

"Ms. Carr, would you mind if we collected a DNA sample and digital print from you? We'd like to test it against what was found in Mr. Tiller's apartment. I have a kit that will allow me to swab your mouth and take your prints. It'll only take a minute or so," Detective Sokolov said.

"That's fine."

"Did you visit Mr. Tiller this past Friday?" Detective Bennie asked. "His phone records show that you two exchanged text messages that day."

"I did. It was in the afternoon."

I opened my mouth, and Detective Sokolov swabbed the inside of my cheek. He then recorded my prints with a digital scanner.

"This afternoon visit, was it another session?" Detective Bennie asked.

"That's correct."

"All done," Detective Sokolov said.

Detective Bennie removed a document from a large envelope and placed it on the storage island.

"We have money transfers from Mr. Tiller's bank account to a PayPal account registered in your name. Each one is for eight thousand dollars."

"Those are payments for my services."

"Pretty expensive," Detective Bennie said.

"He paid by the month. We'd normally do three or four sessions a month."

"I never heard of a dominatrix charging that much," Detective Bennie said as he glanced at his partner.

"I'm good at what I do," I said.

"Did Mr. Tiller make strange noises during your sessions at his apartment, like moaning sounds?"

"Well, sometimes he'd have a gag ball in his mouth and make noises. I guess you could call it moaning. I never saw it that way. Why?"

"We have a witness who heard strange noises from the apartment."

"You must be talking about Barbara, Ms. Ezra. She lives below him. I always wondered if she heard stuff."

Detective Bennie placed a few more documents on the island. I recognized the emails right away. I should have created a separate account for him.

"These emails are from you, Ms. Carr. I'll read one. 'Look, asshole, if you don't continue making payments, I'm letting everyone in town know you're a whiny little boy who likes to be paddled.'" Detective Bennie looked up at me. "Ms. Carr, you're threatening to embarrass Mr. Tiller unless he continues making monetary payments. Any judge would view this as blackmail."

I let out a dismissive breath. "You don't think I'm serious, do you? People say stuff like this all the time."

Detective Bennie read another email. "'Don't ignore me. Pay up. Remember, I also videotaped some of our sessions.'"

"Sounds serious to me," Detective Sokolov said. "Now would be a good time to explain your side of the story, so we don't assume the worst."

"It's getting stuffy in this closet. Let's go back to the living room," I suggested.

The detectives collected their paperwork and followed me. In the living room, I sat back down on my chair and gestured for them to take the couch.

"I first met Errol in New York while I was a full-time dominatrix. He was in town for a meeting and booked a session with me. He loved it. So whenever he visited, he'd see me."

"How often was that?" Sokolov asked.

"I would say about four or five times a year. But I had been a dominatrix for years and wanted something new. That's when I told Errol I decided to retire. He begged me not to, to see only him if I was tired of the daily grind. I told him four sessions a year wouldn't pay my bills. That's when he suggested I become his personal dominatrix."

"Like a personal trainer or chef?" Detective Sokolov asked.

"Yes, just like that. He offered to keep me on a retainer, and I would service him four times a month. I'd have to move to San Francisco for this arrangement to work. I was looking for a change, and switching coasts seemed a good way to start."

"So the eight thousand was your retainer fee?"

"Yes. Errol made the down payment on this apartment and got me set up here. The retainer was enough to cover the mortgage and my living expenses."

"So this is the agreement you're talking about in your emails?"

"Yes. I always knew Errol could change his mind and stop funding me. We had a verbal agreement but nothing in writing. So once I got out here, I worked hard to generate income another way."

I went over to my desk to retrieve my laptop and navigated to my website. "I have an online candle business. It's growing steadily, and I'm on track to match the money Errol gave me. I'm not quite there yet."

"So you were planning on getting out of the arrangement," Detective Sokolov said.

"Sure, but Errol beat me to it. A few months ago, he told me he would only pay my normal session fee, which is six hundred dollars. That pissed me off. I'd done a lot for him. These sessions would sometimes last three hours. And he had this weird thing where he would want me waiting inside his apartment when he came home from work. Like I had broken into his place. Can you believe that? Sometimes I'd be waiting for an hour. He was a difficult client to deal with, and I earned every single penny. So, of course, I argued with him about our agreement. One thing led to another, and it ended up with those emails. So yeah, I wanted him to hold up his end of the deal. I held up my end of the bargain. He needed to do the same."

"So why see him again on Friday if he wasn't following through on your agreement?" Detective Bennie asked.

"Because he begged me and said if I did the session he would hold up his end of the deal, and give me all the backpay he owed me. So I agreed, but after the session he gave me some bullshit about needing a few days to get the money. I knew right then he was lying."

"You sound angry about this," Detective Sokolov said.

"Of course, I was angry. The mortgage on this place is four thousand a month."

"Angry enough to kill Mr. Tiller?"

"What? You think I killed him?"

Neither one answered me. These sons of bitches were building a case against me.

"I'm not saying another word without a lawyer. I'd like you both to leave right now."

I walked over to my front door and held it open.

Detective Sokolov left a business card on my desk. "When you retain counsel, please call so we can arrange another meeting at the station. Oh, one more thing. You wouldn't happen to know where Mr. Tiller's dog is, would you?"

"Get out!"

Chapter Thirty-Three

Peggy

I can't wait to fire his sorry ass.

Darrel was supposed to be in by eight sharp. He had called ahead and said he would be fifteen minutes late because of traffic. I didn't care. As far as I was concerned, if Ray and I could get our butts in on time, so could Darrel.

While I waited outside the building for Darrel to show, the two detectives who had ruined my Sunday showed up.

I told them to stop by in the afternoon. What are they doing here in the morning?

"Good morning, detectives. I thought you were stopping by in the afternoon to question Geneva."

"Good morning. We're actually here to speak to Helen Carr. Do you know her?" Detective Sokolov asked.

"Sure, I know Helen. I can run you up to her apartment right now."

"We appreciate it."

I didn't really care why they wanted to speak to Helen. I was more concerned with catching Darrel outside so I could talk to him privately. I had always thought Guy was listening in on my conversations in my office. I ran those detectives up to

Helen's apartment, dropped them off in front of her door, and left as quickly as possible. As soon as I returned to the lobby, I spotted Darrel outside smoking a cigarette.

"Darrel, you got a minute to chat? Let's take a walk."

"What's up, Peggy?"

"A little birdie told me you're spreading rumors about Errol and me."

"Oh, okay. I know what this is about. Are you talking about them detectives? I ain't told them nothing that isn't true."

"Screw you, Darrel! You have no idea what you're talking about. You better keep your mouth shut if you don't have all the facts."

"All I know is I saw you come out of Mr. Tiller's apartment, your hair is in a tangle, and your cheeks are red. You were smiling like a girl that just got her box chowed."

"You think you're so clever. I know you were the one selling Errol his coke. How about I share that with the police? How would that look for a felon, huh?"

"Peggy, you are so dumb. I already told them about that. I pretty much got immunity."

"Oh, do you?"

"Yeah, go ahead and tell them. Make a fool of yourself. I don't care."

"You know what you don't have immunity from? Me firing you. Not so talkative now, are we?" I sing-songed that last bit just to rub it in even more.

"You can't fire me. Ray's my boss."

"Yeah, and guess who Ray's boss is? Moi." I tapped my finger on my chest. "So it looks like you are F-I-R-E-D. Do you want me to repeat it for you?"

"Nah, I like the sound of me showing up to your home and telling your husband that Mr. Tiller has been feeding you his sausage for the last six months."

"You wouldn't dare!" I seethed.

"Try me."

"Errol's dead, so it's your word against mine. You think my husband will listen to you?"

"I'm a gambling man. I like my odds."

I wanted to slap that silly smirk off Darrel's face, but I couldn't. I had to play this smart. The last thing I wanted was this idiot talking to Ross.

"Look, Darrel, we both have more to lose the longer these cops investigate Errol's death. We both can end up defending ourselves in court. You more than me."

"What do you mean by that?"

"The longer they keep investigating, the greater the chances of my business and your business coming out. You have motive because you were selling him cocaine. And I heard you weren't getting paid. For all I know, you threw him over the railing."

"Man, I didn't do shit. And plus, you have motive too. You guys were screwing. Maybe you got jealous because Mr. Tiller had another piece of action on the side. Or maybe you wanted some money from him."

"Whatever. You're still in jeopardy of losing your job. Ray would fire you for selling cocaine on the premises and lying about your criminal record. So it's best for us both that this investigation goes away. I'll keep my mouth shut so long as you keep your mouth shut. Do we have a deal?"

I stuck my hand out.

"Man, I can't believe I'm cutting a deal with your bony ass."

Darrel shook my hand just as the two detectives stepped out of the building.

"Are you two making up over something?" Detective Sokolov asked.

"I just got done telling Darrel what a great job he's doing here," I said.

"Yeah, Peggy said I was getting a spot bonus of fifty dollars. Ain't that right, Peggy?" Darrel held out his hand.

"Darrel, the petty cash is in my office. I'll give it to you once we're inside. Detectives, everything going okay with Helen?"

"It's fine. We'll see you later."

"What did they mean about seeing you later?" Darrel asked as soon as the detectives were out of earshot.

"They're looking for Errol's dog. Listen, Darrel. I'm dead serious. If we keep our mouths shut, we'll get out of this without a scratch."

"Wait, why are the police talking to Ms. Carr?" Darrel asked. "She lives on the other side of the building. No way she could have heard him fall."

"I don't know, but now that you mention it, I'm curious."

"Hey, maybe Mr. Tiller was screwing her, too."

"You think?"

"I think if you believe you were the only one hopping into his bed, then you're dumber than I thought."

"Have you seen them together?"

"No."

"Speak of the devil. There goes Helen right now."

Helen had just walked out of the building and climbed into a taxi. I waved at her as she rode past.

"You know what we should do?" I said as I turned back to Darrel.

"What's that?"

"We should take a peek around her apartment."

"No way. That's breaking and entering."

"I have a key. No one is breaking in."

"It's the same thing, Peggy. I'm not doing it."

"Sheesh, Darrel. Grow a pair, will you? I'm just asking that you keep watch in case she returns quickly."

"How long you plan to be in there?"

"I don't know, but if she comes back, give me a ring and I'll get out."

"Man, for someone who just said we should keep our noses clean, you got a funny way of doing that."

"Clearly, the police know something about Helen that we don't know. There might be a way for us to keep steering them in that direction. Now man up."

"Screw you."

Chapter Thirty-Four

Jill

IT WAS ANOTHER MONDAY MORNING, another week ahead. The kids were no livelier during breakfast than they had been at dinner last night. I figured until we got through this, it was to be expected. I still struggled with how we ended up where we did. I thought seeing Errol fall was the big secret. Now I find out my son is possibly involved in a blackmail scheme that could have pushed Errol to commit suicide, and it's because he was a Peeping Tom.

Just the thought of that getting out gave me a migraine. I couldn't imagine Ollie being branded a pervert. It would absolutely break my heart, because I knew my son was a good boy. He wasn't a freak. And, of course, there would also be fallout affecting Mia. She didn't deserve any of it. She was innocent in all of this. Was I overthinking things? Perhaps. But it could happen if the police got involved.

What made it worse was the feeling that I was living a double life. Alan and I were no better. Our peeping would come out as well if the police investigated our connections to Errol. What would that do to my standing in the community? I was involved with several charities. Plus, I was one of the most active moms in the PTA. And Alan—what would it mean for his firm? They could lose clients over this, or worse, Alan could be forced out. Seeing Tiller fall was the tip of the iceberg.

A knock on the front door pulled me from my thoughts. It was Helen, and her face wasn't exactly projecting "good morning."

"Helen, is everything okay?" I asked.

"No, it's not," she said as she walked inside and headed straight for the kitchen. "I just got done speaking to the police. They think I had something to do with Errol's death."

"What? Why would they think that?"

Helen remained quiet.

"Helen?" I lowered my head so I could catch her eyes with mine. "What is it?"

"We've been friends for a few years now, haven't we?"

"Yes, of course. You're my dearest friend."

"Right. So, I've been keeping something from you. I don't know why I never told you this. It's not a big deal to me... I used to be a dominatrix when I lived in New York."

I let out a laugh.

"What's so funny?"

"You think I care that you were a dominatrix? Well, at least it explains the latest fragrance in your candle line, Whipping Boy. You know, you didn't have to fib and tell me you worked in public relations."

"Honey, when I said I worked in PR, I meant personal relations. But I know it was stupid to have kept this from you. There's more, though. Errol was a client of mine."

"You're joking." My mouth fell slightly open.

"I'm not. And now the police think I have something to do with his death."

"Do you?"

"Of course not. You have to believe me."

"Okay, I believe you." I poured Helen a cup of coffee. "But why would they come to that conclusion?"

"Because I sent Errol threatening emails that look like I wanted to blackmail him. And I stupidly gave him another session that Friday so the police know I was in his apartment."

I was absolutely flabbergasted as I listened to Helen explain. It was as if she was privy to our entire family discussion last night. The similarities between what she had done and what Ollie and Grant did were staggering. The reason for the threats may have been different, but Helen's plan had been exactly the same as Grant's: force Errol to do something on threat of exposure.

The obvious dawned on me right then.

Errol had received similar threats from two separate parties at about the same time. Surely this could have been the final spiral in his life that prompted him to throw himself off his balcony. I could see the prosecutor in the courtroom making the case: "Errol would still be alive today if it weren't for these individuals bullying him."

Blackmailing Errol only looked one way: bad. Helen was my best friend. Grant was Ollie's best friend. The police could quickly come to the conclusion that we had conspired together. Only we didn't end up getting what we wanted because Tiller jumped.

"Jill, I'm worried that the police will arrest me for blackmail, and I'll end up being the fall guy for Errol's death."

That was one way for this scenario to play out. If we could convince the police that Ollie wasn't involved, or even Grant, Helen would look like the guilty party.

Wait, why am I thinking this? Helen's my best friend. ...And Ollie's your son, Jill. If you had to pick one...

"Wait, let's not jump to conclusions, Helen. Let's think this through. You had an agreement with Errol, and he was backing out. That would put you in a financial crunch, right?"

"That's right. I mean, the candle business helps, but yeah."

"Okay, but my point is there was some financial hardship."

"That's correct."

"From what I know, verbal agreements are still agreements. All you were trying to do was hold Errol to his part of the agreement."

"Damn right. I wasn't letting him get away with it."

"And the threats you made, clearly they were made from a place of momentary anger. I think anyone could see that. People say stuff all the time in the heat of the moment."

"That's exactly what I told the police," Helen said as she pointed at me.

"And plus, you're cooperating with them."

"Yes, I answered all their questions and even allowed them to test my DNA."

"The more truthful you are, the less they'll think you had anything to do with his death. They still have to prove you were in his apartment at the time that he fell."

"You're right, but..." Helen looked off to the side.

I knew that move. "What is it?"

Helen bit her lower lip before letting out a breath. "There is one thing I didn't tell the police. I had a key to Errol's apartment. I used it sometimes to set up his sessions."

"Oh. Well, that sort of flips the script."

"It does, right? I'm screwed."

"Do you still have the key?"

"I do. I never gave it back because I forgot I had it, and then when I remembered I had it, I decided to keep it just in case. You think I should return it to his apartment? Maybe leave it someplace, like in the dresser drawer or something?"

"You can't now. That apartment is one big crime scene. Does anyone else know you have the key?"

"I don't think so."

"I would just throw it away and forget you ever had it. It'll be like it never happened."

"That could work. Okay, I'll do that."

"What about another dominatrix? Did Errol see other people?"

"I don't think he did. He was paying me a lot of money to service him. It would be stupid to keep me on retainer and see another professional."

"People do stupid stuff."

Boy, did I know. All I had to do was look at what Ollie did, or even Alan. They both spied on Ms. Martin and saved proof of their actions. They didn't think it was a big deal at the time, but Errol's death had made a mess out of everything. I honestly didn't believe Helen had anything physical to do with Errol dying. It takes a particular type of person to push another person over a balcony, and that wasn't Helen. But I also couldn't be certain her emails hadn't affected him mentally.

"Did the police mention a break-in at Errol's apartment?" I asked.

"No, but they wanted my DNA so they could cross-check it against other DNA found in the apartment."

"How many different DNA samples were found?"

"I'm not sure. Why?"

"If Errol was murdered, then someone visited him after you. Try to think back to that Friday. Did he mention anything about guests coming over later, or recent visitors, or maybe he was complaining about something?"

Helen opened her mouth, and I waited for an answer that would shift the investigation back to Grant and Ollie.

"Our conversations were always about our deal," she said.

I kept my composure as a wave of relief passed through my body. Of course, I didn't want my son mixed up in this mess, but Helen was also my friend. I had to try and help her. I just had to do it in a way that didn't involve telling her about Grant and Ollie. At least not yet.

Chapter Thirty-Five

Jill

HELEN HAD some candle issues she had to deal with, so she didn't stick around very long. As I watched her leave, I couldn't help but feel incredibly guilty that I was withholding information that may or may not have helped her. But this was my family I was talking about; I had a duty to protect them. Plus, I reasoned, Helen couldn't have killed Errol. She might have been guilty of blackmail, but she was not a murderer.

I believed whoever killed Errol had to have vile hate for him. Pushing someone over a balcony is personal, especially if it involves a struggle. It's like choking someone. You're there, staring at the person's face as their life slips away. It takes a certain type of person to kill someone in such an intimate fashion. Helen was not that person.

And this person needed access. If there were no signs of a break-in, then Errol must have known his killer. They would have had to gain access to the building, which wasn't that difficult. The doorman was only there during the day, and people hold the door open for strangers all the time—though it would be easier for someone who lived in the building. That actually didn't help Helen's case, especially since she had a key to the apartment. But what did it all mean for Ollie and Grant?

Grant lived in the Residence and could move around the building freely. Ollie claimed to know nothing of the emails until after Grant had sent them—that plan was all Grant's doing. They were both away camping when Errol died, so neither could have pushed him. But were there other emails, more damaging ones? Was Grant able to convince Ollie to conspire with him further? If there was one thing I knew about my son, it was that he was a giving person. He'd do anything to help a friend.

I was going around in circles. Talking to Kelly Walker might shed light on the situation. I knew Alan was against any contact with her for now. It could make the situation worse and complicate matters. Our sons may have been best friends, but we weren't. I didn't hang out with Kelly like I did with Helen. Sure, we invited the Walkers to our holiday parties, but we weren't planning vacations with them.

I sent Alan a text message asking if he had an appointment with the lawyer. He answered a few minutes later, saying he had just confirmed an afternoon meeting. Just having the appointment made me feel better; hearing what the lawyer had to say could alleviate my concern and stop my overthinking.

My mind wandered back to Kelly. Surely, she must know what Grant did. Neither Alan nor I had bothered to ask Ollie that question. We were too busy processing the whole blackmail thing. But what if Kelly had no idea about any of this? What if Grant lied about approaching his mother about her affair? Because if I had done what Kelly had and Ollie confronted me, I'd be watching his every move like a hawk. Another text message from Alan asked if I wanted to attend the meeting. It was probably best that we present a united front, so I texted back that I would.

A knock on my door caught my attention. I thought maybe Helen had come back, so I didn't bother to look out the window before opening the door.

"Mrs. Jill Pittman?"

"Oh. That's me. Can I help you?"

"My name is Detective Sokolov, and this is Detective Bennie. Mind if we ask you a few questions?"

So that's what it feels like to be punched in the stomach.

"Did something happen to one of my children?"

"No, it's nothing like that. Mind if we come inside?"

Yes.

"Not at all," I said as I held the door open. "Can I offer you two coffee?"

"We're fine, thank you. We're investigating the death of Errol Tiller."

"Yes, I knew Errol. It's so sad."

Why did you offer up that information, Jill? Only answer direct questions from now on.

"Is that so? Could you tell us how you knew Mr. Tiller?"

You see, they didn't know.

"I met him through my charity work. We worked on a couple of fundraisers together."

"So your relationship with him was purely professional?"

"That's right."

Why? What do you know that I don't?

"This is a nice house you have here," Detective Sokolov said as he looked around. "There aren't many houses on Nob Hill. It's mostly apartment buildings."

"Yes, it's one of the reasons we bought it."

"How long ago was that?"

"About two years now."

Stay calm, Jill. They're fishing for information.

Detective Sokolov looked over to the deck off of the kitchen. "You mind if we take a look at the view?"

"Be my guest."

"Wow, look at this view," Detective Bennie said as he stepped onto the deck. "You can see all of the bay. Too bad about that building. It kind of ruins the view a little." He flashed a smile at me. "But not much."

Detective Sokolov spun around, slowly eyeing the deck. He looked up to the balcony off of my bedroom.

"I bet the view up there is just as good," he said.

"It is. May I ask what this is all about? I'm a little confused at the moment."

"I'm sorry. Let me explain. Saturday morning, my partner and I were in Mr. Tiller's apartment." He pointed to the Middle Finger. "He lives in that building on the top floor."

"Yes, so I've gathered."

"Well, Mr. Tiller has a telescope, and I looked through it at Nob Hill. I'm pretty sure I saw a woman looking back at me."

"Surely you're not suggesting it was me?"

"Do you own a telescope?"

"My husband does."

"I don't see it."

"We keep it on our balcony," I said.

"That one up there? Could we take a peek?"

I led them up the stairs and to our balcony. Detective Sokolov made the same slow turning move he'd done on the deck below, only this time, he nodded his head.

"Yes. This is it. It's familiar," he said. "I saw you looking through that telescope."

"I might have, I guess. Sometimes I like to look at the sailboats on the bay."

Detective Sokolov peered through the telescope. After moving it around for a bit, he moved his face away from the eyepiece. "Did you know you can see straight into Mr. Tiller's apartment?"

"You don't say," I said dryly.

"I didn't think we'd find the home on the first try," Detective Bennie said.

"My partner and I had a bet on whether we could find out who was looking through the telescope," Detective Sokolov chimed in.

"Detectives, I'm afraid I still don't see your point here."

"Mrs. Pittman, do you know anyone who lives in that building?"

"My friend Helen Carr lives there."

"We spoke to Ms. Carr this morning. Nice lady."

Did they know Helen was just here? Are they following her? Are they now watching my home?

"Yes, she is."

"Were you aware that Ms. Carr was a practicing dominatrix and Mr. Tiller was her client?"

Lie or tell the truth. Which is it, Jill?

"I was aware." I straightened defensively. "Work is work."

"Yes, we agree. We're not concerned with her profession; we're interested in her relationship with Mr. Tiller. We're slowly learning that Mr. Tiller saw a lot of women."

"I can tell you their relationship was completely professional. Nothing more."

"And what about your relationship with Mr. Tiller?"

"I'm offended at the implication. I'm a happily married woman."

"I apologize, Mrs. Pittman. We're just trying to learn as much as possible about Mr. Tiller."

"I don't see how any of this helps."

"Is Mia Pittman your daughter?"

"Yes. Why do you ask?"

"She worked at Tiller & Associates, didn't she?"

"She completed an internship there this summer, yes. Why are you asking about Mia?"

"Well, this is actually why we stopped by. During her employment at Tiller & Associates, your daughter filed a sexual harassment complaint against Mr. Tiller."

"What?"

"I take it you weren't aware of this."

"No, I wasn't." I pressed my hand against my chest to calm my breathing.

"We read through the complaint. The harassment was verbal, not physical. But we'd like to ask Mia a few questions about the incident."

"Well, she's in school right now."

"Yes, of course. Is it possible for you to bring her to the station after? Or, if it's easier, we can swing by here again. We only have a few questions. It won't take long."

"Uh, yes. That's fine. I'll pick her up from school, and we'll come to the station."

Detective Sokolov handed me a card. "If you could call when you're on the way? We appreciate your cooperation, Mrs. Pittman."

Chapter Thirty-Six

Jill

I was still in a state of shock after the police left my home. I couldn't believe Mia had been harboring this horrible secret. And to think, all last night, we were discussing Errol and harping on Ollie for what he did. She must have felt terrible, knowing what kind of person he was but not feeling like she could say something.

Why would she not tell us?

For the first time since I had heard about Errol's death, I was happy he was dead. Fricking ecstatic. I was so angry and hurt that Mia had to endure this crap from that bastard. She was a teenager, for God's sake. What kind of man says sexual things to a girl at that age? I understood how Grant must have felt after finding out Errol was sleeping with his mother: rage. I didn't blame the kid. He wanted to protect his mother. That's what families do—they protect each other.

I sent a text to Mia telling her I would pick her up from school and to wait for me. Then I called Alan.

"Hey, what's up?" he said.

"Alan, I just had a visit from the police."

"The police? Why were the police there?"

"It's a long story, so I'll cut to the important part. I just found out that bastard sexually harassed our daughter."

"Who did?"

"Errol did. Mia filed a report at work because of him."

"Why didn't she say something to us?"

"I don't know, but the police said it was verbal, not physical. You know what? I'm glad that son of a bitch is dead. I'm filled with joy."

"So wait, the police came to the house to tell you that?"

I realized then I had never told Alan that I looked into Errol's apartment exactly as one of the detectives was looking through his telescope. I quickly recapped the situation for him.

"You guys looked at each other at the exact same time?"

"I know, it's crazy, but it happened... Oh, my God. Do you think Errol spied on Mia from his apartment?"

"Well, if the detective could see you looking at him, it's possible."

"Ugh, so disgusting. She's only a teenager."

"Did they mention anything about the emails from Grant?"

"No. They probably don't know."

"Yet. They'll find them if they keep digging. It's good that I got the meeting with the lawyer set up."

"Alan, it's starting to look like we did something. What if the police think we already knew about Errol sexually harassing Mia? And then they find out about the emails blackmailing him and tie it back to Ollie? It could look like we—you and me, and Ollie and Grant—schemed to blackmail Errol. Us to punish him for what he did to Mia, and Grant to get him to stop screwing his mother."

"Let's remain level-headed here. We still need to hear what the lawyer has to say."

"Should we tell him everything?"

"I think we have to."

"I mean, obviously, the thing with Ollie and Mia, but what about us?"

"Ollie is the most exposed, but we can mention Mia's harassment report. As for our peeping, I don't see how it's relevant right now."

"I'm worried that the police will seriously think we colluded with Grant to get back at Errol."

"Stop, Jill. First off, the police have to place one of us there. Ollie has a rock-solid alibi; he was camping with Grant. Mia was at her friend's house. And I was out with clients."

"I don't have an alibi," I said. "No one can vouch for me being home alone all night."

"Jill, you are the last person the police would suspect. We'll tell the lawyer everything, so he has the full picture, and then we'll decide. Honestly, I think they're doing exactly what you said they were doing. They're grasping for anything to sink their hooks into. They want this to be a murder investigation, but it's a suicide. And if for some reason I'm wrong, the killer is most likely someone in the building. Easy access, right?"

I drew a deep breath. "You'll need to go to the meeting alone. I texted Mia that I'll be picking her up after school. The detectives want to ask her a few questions about the report she filed."

"Does she know?"

"No. I'll tell her when I see her."

"That's fine. I'll deal with the lawyer, and we'll touch base later. Okay?"

"Okay."

"I love you. Everything will be fine."

"Love you too."

I appreciated Alan's confidence in the matter. I sometimes wished I were more like him. He didn't overthink, he was decisive, and he lived with the end result. My fear of the outcome was often what paralyzed me. But one thing I was confident of was that there was nothing I wouldn't do to protect this family. Nothing.

Chapter Thirty-Seven

Kelly

THE POSITIVE CHANGE in Grant's mood had stuck with him through the night. He was talkative over breakfast and even hugged me before heading off to school. I was really beginning to believe things were returning to normal.

Ever since he came home, I'd told myself to remain calm and not get excited. Grant could snap back into his old ways, and I didn't want to set myself up for disappointment. But seeing him across the dining table smiling at me while he ate his cereal made my heart full.

Let's just see how things go when he comes home from school.

I was a stay-at-home mom and ran a tiny graphic design business from the apartment. Most months, I had two or three projects. It kept me busy throughout the day and made me feel productive. That month, I had only one task to deal with: a brochure. But my distractions with Grant were making it challenging to finish. I found myself procrastinating at the drop of a hat. Anything and everything was a reason to shut my laptop.

Kent had left for work earlier, so as soon as Grant was out the door, I told myself I would finish designing that brochure no matter what. I fixed myself a cup of green tea and settled at the dining table. No sooner had I opened the laptop than I heard a knock on the door. I thought it must have been Grant coming back because he had forgotten something. I rushed to open the door.

"Hello, are you Mrs. Kelly Walker?" asked a man in a suit.

"I am."

"I'm Detective Sokolov, and this is Detective Bennie. Do you have a moment to answer a few questions for us?"

My heart skipped a beat.

"Questions about what?"

"We're investigating the death of Errol Tiller. Your cooperation would be helpful."

"It's a terrible thing that happened to him. Please, come inside. Can I offer you anything to drink?"

"No, thank you."

I pushed my laptop out of the way, and all three of us sat at the dining table.

"How would you describe your relationship with Mr. Tiller?" Detective Sokolov asked as soon as he took a seat.

"My relationship? I wouldn't call being cordial in the lobby a relationship. He seemed like a nice person, though."

Detective Bennie placed a paper on the table and slid it over to me. It was a photograph of me kissing Errol on his balcony—the same one Grant had confronted me with.

"Seems like there was a bit more to it than being cordial in the lobby," Detective Bennie said.

As I stared at the photograph, one thing came to mind: the Pittman boy, Ollie. He was Grant's best friend. The Pittmans lived on Nob Hill. I'd been to their place a few times and knew they had a view of the building. I'd always wondered how Grant found out about Errol and me. Now, it occurred to me: It must have been Ollie.

"I was having an affair. So what? You think that has something to do with Errol's death?"

"Could you tell us how serious your relationship was with Mr. Tiller?"

"It was sex, nothing more. I broke it off about a month and a half ago."

"What caused the breakup?"

"I'm married. It was a fling. Don't overthink it."

"Well, that's sort of our job. Was Mr. Tiller surprised by the breakup, or was it just a fling for him, too?"

"He wasn't heartbroken about it, if that's what you're asking."

"When was the last time you were in Mr. Tiller's apartment?"

"When I broke up with him."

"Was there any contact since then...maybe a phone call or a text message?"

"A few. He kept asking to meet one last time. I refused, though."

"How did he take it?"

"He seemed angry, but that wasn't my problem."

"Do you think he was angry enough to tell your husband?"

I took a moment to think about that question, because it had been a viable concern when I called off the relationship with Errol. I had always thought he was the type who would threaten to do something like that—not to get me to come back to him, but because he was petty.

"It was a concern, but if I continued to see him, my husband would eventually find out. So that was a possibility no matter what I did. Look, I made a mistake and I have to live with it. But if you're here to find out if I had anything to do with his death, I didn't. I don't know anything about his personal life, and we never talked much. Our relationship was purely sexual and nothing more. It's as if our relationship was as simple as a wave in the lobby, because I knew nothing about him and didn't care to."

"I have to ask," Detective Sokolov said. "Did you visit Mr. Tiller on the day he died?"

"No."

"Our tech guys back at the lab found an email sent to Mr. Tiller," Detective Bennie said as he slid another paper toward me. "They were able to trace the IP address to your apartment. The photograph of you and Mr. Tiller was attached to the email, and the message reads: 'Stay away or else.' Are you sure your husband doesn't know?" Detective Bennie asked.

I was speechless. Could Kent have known all this time? Grant had told me he didn't say anything to his father. Did he lie to me?

"I—I'm not sure. I didn't think he knew. Are you sure the email was sent from here? Because it looks like the picture was taken from a distance. Errol's apartment faces Nob Hill."

"We're certain the email came from the apartment. If our tech guys examine all the devices in the home, they can figure out which one sent the email. We were hoping to avoid that and ask you."

Could Ollie have sent it? He could have visited Grant when I wasn't here and used our Wi-Fi. Maybe Grant has no idea this email was sent. ...Kelly, stop. You already know who sent it.

"Mrs. Walker?"

"Huh?" I looked up from the photo, still deep in thought.

"I asked you if you recognized the sender's email address. Could it be your husband's email?"

"It's not. I don't recognize that email."

"Who else lives here besides you and your husband?"

"It's just us and our son, Grant."

Detective Bennie nodded. "I see. Did your son know about the relationship?"

I sighed. "He did. In fact, he's the reason I stopped seeing Errol. I promised him I would. But I don't think he would have sent this email. It's out of character."

"Kids tend to act out," Detective Sokolov said. "Your son's not in any trouble. We're just trying to get the facts straight."

"Well, if you want to get the facts straight, you need to talk to the person who took that picture."

"Do you know who took it?"

I had been so mortified when Grant approached me about my relationship with Errol that I didn't ask where the photograph came from. But it had to have been Ollie who took it and gave it to Grant. He was the troublemaker here.

"I have a hunch, detectives. Ollie Pittman is my son's best friend, and he lives on Nob Hill. And he's into photography."

The two detectives gave each other a look. "Is his mother Jill Pittman?"

"Yes, she is. Are you talking to her, as well?"

"Does Ollie come over here often?"

"Often enough that he could have sent that email. The more I think about it, the more I think he took that picture."

"There were a couple of follow-up emails," Detective Bennie said as he produced more sheets of paper. "They make the same threat. Mrs. Walker, we'd like to ask your son questions about these emails, just so we have all the facts straight."

"Why? I just told you, Ollie Pittman probably took that picture."

"And we appreciate that information, but we still have some questions for your son. We'd like to find out who sent the emails."

"I already told you, it was probably Ollie. But Grant's in school now, so we would have to arrange a meeting later."

"Your cooperation is appreciated," Detective Sokolov said as he handed me his card. "You can bring your son to the station, or we can meet here, if you prefer. Just let us know what you decide."

Just when I thought things in this family were getting back to normal.

As soon as the detectives left, I headed into Grant's room. His laptop was gone, because he had taken it to school. I searched his desk drawer for anything that would signal he had done this.

What was I thinking? I knew Grant did it. I just didn't want to believe it. I had come so close to putting this mess with Errol behind us, and now these stupid emails had pulled me right back into it. Once again, I was in danger of Kent finding out the truth.

I searched Grant's room (and even went through the pockets of his dirty clothes) but found nothing. Would there even be physical evidence? If Grant sent those emails, the evidence would be on his laptop or cell phone. I dropped down to the floor and looked under his bed. Aside from a T-shirt and an old candy bar wrapper, there was nothing. I pulled back his comforter and stared at his sheets for a moment before lifting up his pillow. Underneath was a folded piece of paper. I unfolded it and recognized Grant's handwriting right away. The heading read: Top Ways to Kill Errol Tiller.

Chapter Thirty-Eight

Alan

My MEETING with the lawyer was scheduled for two in the afternoon. Larry Burke had been a client at the firm for the past five years, and we'd become friendly during that time. So when I called him asking for his advice, he was more than willing to meet with me.

"Alan, good to see you," he said as he greeted me in the waiting room.

Larry was a partner at a reasonably large firm in the city. They were well known and had a good track record in defending their clients. Larry led me into a corner office and motioned for me to have a seat as he swung around to the other side of his desk.

"Can I get you anything to drink? Coffee, sparkling water...?"

"Nah, I'm fine."

"Okay then, let's get into your concerns."

"As I mentioned briefly, Ollie has himself mixed up in something that we're not sure we should be concerned about or not."

"Yep, yep. Tell me everything you know as best you can."

I started by telling Larry about Ollie taking photos of Ms. Martin alone, and of her having sex with Mr. Tiller.

"This was done from his bedroom with a camera, correct?"

"Yeah. Last year, I bought him a really good lens. It pretty much puts you right into her apartment."

"Okay, so this is simple. Ollie wasn't on Ms. Martin's private property when looking inside her apartment, so no crime was committed."

"What about the photographs?"

"Again, photographing something or someone on private property, in this case Ms. Martin, while being on public property is legal, even from your home. If she did find out, she could make a complaint to the police, but nothing would come of it unless it could be proven that Ollie's actions placed Ms. Martin in danger. I'm not hearing that. What else is there?"

"Some of the photos were used to threaten Errol Tiller."

"Tiller is the man who fell from his balcony?"

"That's the one. Ollie's best friend is a boy named Grant Walker. He lives in the same building as Errol. Ollie happened to snap a picture of Errol making out with Grant's mom on his balcony."

"You know, Ollie might have a great career as a paparazzo," Larry joked.

"I'll keep that in mind," I said dryly. "So anyway, being the friend he is, he sends Grant the photograph. Grant emails the photograph to Errol, telling him to leave his mother alone or else."

"Or else what?"

"That's it, just 'or else.'"

"Well, that's very vague. Or else he'll tickle him? Slap a drink out of his hand? Spit in his food? You get my point."

"Yes."

"Was Ollie party to this email?"

"He had no idea until after the fact."

"Okay, so Ollie committed no crime here. What else?"

"Ollie also sent Grant the photos of Errol having sex with Ms. Martin. Grant then sent another email telling Errol to leave his mother alone, or he would upload the posts to the internet."

"Okay, now the intent is clear. This is blackmail, as simple as that. Was Ollie party to this?"

"No, he found out after. He swears he had no idea Grant would do that."

"When Ollie gave Grant the photos of Errol having sex with this other woman, was this after he found out that Grant had emailed Errol the photo of him with his mother?"

"Ollie found out about the emails after both of them were already sent."

"Okay. I don't believe Ollie has committed any crimes here. He could be named an accomplice if he had helped craft the email, or even if he suggested the idea to Grant. The prosecution would have to prove that. I don't think you have anything to worry about so far."

"That's a relief, because one more thing worries Jill and me. Our daughter did an internship at Errol's company. Unbeknownst to us, she filed a sexual harassment report against him to the company's HR. Apparently, he was making some unwelcome remarks."

"How did you find out about this? From Mia?"

"The police, they came over...it's a long story."

"Tell me."

I quickly explained how the detective had seen Jill on her balcony and, on a lark, came over to question her.

"Sounds like they're wasting their time."

"Jill and I are worried that these tiny connections between Errol and us could be brought together and turned into something more."

"It's perfectly normal to think this, but nothing I have heard so far says that you guys killed Errol. And let's be honest, that's why you're here. You don't want to catch a bad break and get wrongly blamed for Errol's death."

"Exactly."

"Did you conspire in any way with any of these other people to do bodily harm to Errol Tiller?"

"No. God, no."

"Then you have nothing to worry about. The person who has the most to worry about is Grant, and even that's a stretch. What SFPD is trying to determine right now is whether there was foul play involved with Tiller's death. If there isn't, they rule his death as either accidental or suicide. That's why they're poking around. It's not necessarily because they think he was murdered."

"And you don't think the emails could make them think there was foul play?"

"It's not enough. Look, if Grant made violent threats against Tiller, the police would need evidence of Grant being in Tiller's apartment within a time that coincides with the time Tiller fell."

"He was camping with my son all weekend."

"Then he has nothing to worry about."

I drew a deep breath and exhaled as I rubbed my palms against my pants. "Larry, I gotta tell you, I feel much better after talking with you."

"I'm glad to hear that. If anything else develops, feel free to give me a call."

Chapter Thirty-Nine

Jill

WAITING in the pick-up line at Mia's school, I still couldn't get over the fact that Errol had sexually harassed my daughter. I wished he were alive just so I could punch him in the face. I bet his office didn't do a damn thing about Mia's complaint because he was the owner. It was probably filed away to collect dust. I made a mental note to myself to get a copy of that report. Maybe if we showed it to a lawyer, we would have some recourse against his company. As far as I knew, it was still in business.

At 3:15 sharp, I spotted Mia coming out of the main building. I waved my arm frantically inside my car, hoping she would see it. I was about to toot the horn when she spotted my car.

"Hi, Mom," she said as she climbed inside.

"Hi, sweetie. How was school?" I started the engine and pulled away from the curb.

"It was okay. Wait, is Ollie coming?"

"No, he has his photography club meeting today."

"Oh, yeah."

"So, Mia, I wanted to pick you up because we need to talk about something."

"Aw, Mom. Please don't tell me this is more about last night."

"It sort of is. Mia, I know about the complaint you filed against Mr. Tiller during your internship."

"Oh."

"Mia, why didn't you come to me or your father about this?"

"Because I didn't want to make a big deal about it."

"But it is a big deal, Mia. It was sexual harassment. And it's a problem at a lot of companies."

"I know, Mom. I hear inappropriate remarks everywhere there are men."

My second punch in the stomach for the day.

"You do?"

"Mom, come on. You're acting like you live in a cave."

"Okay, but it still doesn't make it right, and it's especially wrong when it's your boss."

"I know. That's why I reported it to Human Resources."

"What did Errol do to you?"

"He didn't touch me or anything like that. He just kept making comments. At first, they were innocent enough, like 'cute skirt.' But then he got more aggressive and would want to know if I was dating anyone or what kind of boys I liked. He even asked if I was a virgin."

"He *what*? That bastard!"

"Calm down, Mom. I'm a big girl. I can handle this stuff."

"But are you? Still a virgin?" I stole a glance in her direction.

"Yes, Mom!"

"Okay, okay. I'm proud of you, Mia, for sticking up for yourself, especially against the company owner. Don't let anyone mistreat you, no matter who they are."

"Thanks, Mom. So how did you find out?"

"The police came over this morning."

"Why?"

"Because I was being nosy on the day Errol died. I was looking at his apartment with one of your father's telescopes. Turns out Errol owns one too, and the detective happened to be looking through it and spotted me."

"Are you serious?"

"I swear. That and the issue about you is why they visited. They asked a few questions about how I knew Errol, since I mentioned I did."

"Did they ask about Ollie?"

"No. And if anyone, especially the police, asks about Ollie or anything we discussed last night, you don't say anything."

"You want me to lie?"

"I want you to be quiet. Your father is, as we speak, consulting with a lawyer regarding Ollie's situation."

"Oh, my God. Is it that serious?"

"We're just taking precautions."

"Mom, do you think Ollie had anything to do with Mr. Tiller's death?"

"No, of course not. Plus, your brother was away on a camping trip. Why? Do you know something we don't?"

"No, I'm just asking. I don't think Ollie was involved in what happened to Mr. Tiller. But he shouldn't be taking pictures of people in their apartments. It's an invasion of privacy, right?"

"That's right," I mumbled.

I decided not to take Mia straight to the police station for questioning. I wanted to hear what the lawyer had to say first. When we got home, Mia headed straight to her room and I went to mine. I still hadn't heard from Alan regarding the meeting, and it was slowly eating away at me. I sent a text, and he answered that it went well and he was on his way home. I would have liked a bit more detail, but I could wait.

In the meantime, I took a peek at Errol's apartment through the telescope, but I stayed in the bedroom this time. The last thing I wanted was to get caught peeping on his apartment again by Detective Sokolov. The drapes were still open, but nobody was visible inside. I don't know what I had hoped to see. But I knew that, until the police declared Errol's death a suicide and closed the case, I'd always be wary of a knock on my front door.

I stepped onto the balcony, and my thoughts immediately harkened back to that Friday night. I must have replayed that scene of Errol falling in my head at least a hundred times. I distinctly remember seeing him when he was halfway through my field of vision; at least, that's when I consciously noticed him. But what I really wanted to determine was what my peripheral vision saw. If I knew that, I could see if Errol had accidentally fallen, purposely jumped, or been pushed.

What if you determine Errol was pushed? What then, Jill?

That was an excellent question. Knowing that and telling the police would only extend the investigation and have it focus even more on my family, or at the very least, keep us involved. Did I want to invite that trouble into our lives? I already felt like we were scrambling to disconnect Ollie from Errol.

I would have to pretend I didn't know. Everyone lies, right? There are good lies and bad lies. Sometimes it's easy to justify a lie. Even a jury of my peers might agree with my lying.

But could I live with the lie? That was an easy question to answer. If it meant protecting Ollie, I wouldn't think twice. Would I lie for Grant? It would depend on the situation, but most likely not.

It still baffled me how witnessing him fall had led to discovering everyone in my family, even my best friend, had connections to Errol that I had been unaware of. It was odd, and I wasn't even including Kelly Walker in the equation.

I'm dying to know what she knows. Could she be an ally?

Her ears must have been burning, because no sooner had the thought crossed my mind than my cell phone rang. It was Kelly.

She knows. Why else would she be calling now?

I answered the phone. "Kelly, what a nice surprise."

"Hi, Jill. I hope I didn't catch you at a bad time."

"No, not at all. How is everything?"

"Everything is...let's just say my life isn't going as well as it could be. Can we talk in person?"

"Um, yes, sure."

I heard Alan call out from downstairs.

"How about that small coffee shop near your place, say, in an hour?"

"Alan just got home. Let me call you back, and we'll figure out a time, okay?"

Alan appeared just as I disconnected the call.

"Hey," he said, a little out of breath. "Where's Mia? In her room?"

"Yeah."

"And Ollie?"

"Photography club meeting after school."

"How did the questioning go at the police station?"

"I didn't go yet. I thought waiting and hearing what you learned would be better."

"Good idea." Alan sat on the bed's edge, and I sat next to him. "It's all good news, I promise."

He went over everything he had told the lawyer and what the lawyer had said.

"In a nutshell, we have nothing to worry about," Alan said.

"You trust this lawyer? This is our son we're talking about."

185

"I know, and I do. Larry Burke has been with the firm for years, and I've gotten to know him well. We're in good hands."

"I'm so relieved to hear this. I kept thinking he would say we're screwed and have to retain him in case of interrogation and a trial, and..."

"Not yet. Larry said to sit tight, keep our mouths shut, and ride out this investigation. He said if something changes, contact him."

"Something might have changed. I just got a call from Kelly Walker. She wants to talk."

"About what?"

"She didn't say, but I sensed panic in her voice. That's when you came home, and I told her I'd call her back. So, what now? Maybe she knows something that can help us."

"Or she knows something that can hurt us. Larry said not to talk to anyone about this."

"So ignore her?"

"For now, yes."

Chapter Forty

Helen

As soon as I stepped into my apartment, I smelled a scent that didn't belong. I put my purse down and walked around, sniffing different rooms and corners. Sometimes it smelled strong, and sometimes it was barely there. The scent was familiar, but I couldn't quite place it.

I sniffed the sleeve of my blouse, thinking maybe I had brushed up against someone with strong perfume outside, but my clothing smelled normal. I walked into my bedroom and was able to pick it out—just barely, because it fought with my own scent.

It suddenly dawned on me where I knew the scent. It smelled like Shalimar perfume, the kind that Peggy Meyer, the building manager, wore. Why would she be here without my permission? Was it something to do with the building? I hadn't reported a maintenance issue, and anyway, Darrel or Ray would have dealt with that.

My chest tightened as I imagined Peggy walking around my apartment. Could she have been snooping?

I searched my apartment to see if anything had been moved out of place. Nothing seemed to be. I stepped into my bedroom and opened the drawers to my dresser and bedside tables. It didn't look like it had been rummaged through. Lastly, I entered my walk-in closet. My clothes still hung neatly, and my shoes were lined up in the same orderly manner. She could have been here and just been careful about how she touched things. I looked over at the storage island, where I kept my dominatrix clothing and accessories.

I pulled open the top drawer and stared at my leather outfits. I honestly couldn't tell if someone had taken something out and returned it. I opened the second drawer, revealing more of my clothing. The bottom drawer contained accessories, like restraints, gags, whips, paddles, and blindfolds. Also inside that drawer was a velvet-lined box that held my jeweled nipple clamps. That box was also where I kept the key to Errol's apartment.

It was missing. Someone had definitely been in my apartment.

I first thought that the detectives I spoke to had returned to search. Peggy could have let them in and stayed while they searched. It would explain the Shalimar scent. I was no lawyer, but I was pretty sure they would need a warrant to search my place, and I should have been given a copy of it. Plus, I never told them about the key.

My gut told me the police hadn't been inside my apartment. I imagined if they were, my belongings would have been moved around. Whoever took the key had been careful because they knew they weren't supposed to be here.

To have my privacy invaded like that sickened me. It also angered me. I couldn't help but zero in on Peggy as the culprit. It had to be her; I smelled her perfume. Plus, she would recognize the key because she makes all the key copies. But why would she take it? She couldn't have known it was for Errol's apartment, or that I had a copy. For all she knew, it could have been an extra key I kept for my place.

Was it possible that Errol mentioned to her that he'd given me a copy? I doubted he did. And the only person I had told was Jill.

What do I do now? Do I corner Peggy? If I'm wrong about her, I let the cat out of the bag, and she tells the cops. If I report a break-in, I could just say a key was taken, but why would someone break into my place, leave my jewelry, and take a key? All that does is put more attention on me.

I needed a sounding board. I dialed Jill's number and listened to her phone ring, but she wasn't picking up. I sent a text message for her to call me ASAP. I needed to come up with a plan—quick.

Chapter Forty-One

Jill

HELEN HAD CALLED and messaged while Alan and I were talking. She sounded like she really needed to talk, so I called her back quickly, wondering if her situation had escalated. If it had, was that a good thing for Ollie?

The guilt returned. I didn't want to hang Helen out to dry. She was my best friend. I had to figure out how to help her and not make our situation worse. But Alan and I had agreed not to tell anyone. We didn't need anything dividing us at the moment.

I felt like I was being pulled in ten different directions and had to choose one. I told Alan I was visiting Helen and would be back shortly, reassuring him that I would tell her nothing.

Helen met me in the lobby of her building and escorted me back to her apartment. I kept quiet, knowing what she wanted to tell me was something that needed to be discussed behind closed doors.

As soon as she closed the front door behind us, she blurted out, "It's Peggy. I know it's her."

"Who is Peggy?"

"She's the manager of the building. I think she broke into my apartment. Can you smell it? Take a deep breath."

"What am I smelling for?"

"Shalimar. It's the perfume she wears."

Helen walked around her apartment, sniffing the air. "Over here. It's a bit stronger."

She waved at me to come to her. I took a deep breath and then another.

"Can you smell it?" she asked as she eyed me.

"I think so, but why do you suspect it's her?"

"Everyone in the building knows when Peggy's been around because of that perfume. Plus, she has access to all the apartments. She was here. I know it."

I'd never seen Helen like this before. She was always calm and collected. But right then, she looked jittery—spooked, even.

"Okay, let's assume Peggy was in your apartment. What reasons would she have to be here?"

Helen grabbed me by the arm and led me into her bedroom. "She was in my closet."

Helen opened the bottom drawer to the storage island, which was filled with bondage stuff.

"In this box—" she took it out and placed it on top of the island "—I keep nipple clamps. But it's also where I kept the key to Errol's apartment. It's gone. I didn't move it or misplace it. Someone took it."

"And you think it was Peggy?"

"Of course I do. Who else could it be?"

"No maintenance calls?" I asked.

"Nope, and even if I had one, Darrel or Ray would have dealt with it, so why would my apartment smell like Peggy's perfume?"

"Have you thought of asking Peggy?"

"I have, but if I asked her if she was inside my apartment, she could easily deny it, and then she would know I know. I'm telling you, Jill. I know it was Peggy. Maybe Errol told Peggy I had the key because he requested an extra one be made or something. But I don't think he would have done that."

"So she was being nosy and found it," I said. "The odds of that happening... I don't see it."

"I know, but what else could it be? And *why* would she even think to search in the first place?"

"Exactly. She needs a reason to come here," I agreed.

"All I can come up with is that she had another conversation with the police, and they told her that I was a dominatrix and Errol was my client."

"Are you sure you didn't mention the key to the police?"

"I'm sure."

Helen turned away, mumbling to herself. I couldn't believe Peggy had broken into Helen's apartment. Assuming that's what she did, she had abused her position as the building manager. She had committed a crime, and Helen could press charges. I bet the police would find her fingerprints if they looked. But then, Helen would have some awkward explaining to do about the key.

Then something else occurred to me.

"Helen, what if the police didn't mention anything to Peggy?"

"Then what reason would she have to come into my apartment? ...Wait, what if she's searching everyone's apartment? What if she's playing amateur sleuth and hoping to crack the case?"

"I don't think that's what she's doing. I think she's got something to hide. What if she has a connection to Errol that nobody knows about? You know, like your dominatrix thing."

Helen drew a sharp breath. "I never thought of that. She's married, but what if she was screwing Errol?"

"You think that's it?"

"It's got to be. Errol was a skirt chaser. I can't tell you how many times he tried to have sex with me. I denied him each time with a slap to his face. That's the dominatrix in me." Helen smiled.

"And you said she's married, right?" I asked.

"She is. If she were screwing him, she wouldn't want that to come out and risk her husband finding out. Her husband is wealthy and provides a nice life for her."

"I dunno, Helen. The more I think of it, the more likely it sounds."

It was likely because I wanted it to be. I was trying to figure out how to steer the investigation away from my family. Was Peggy doing the same thing and trying to distance herself?

"You know, Helen, if Peggy knew about your side gig, she could have talked to the police about it. And she might be trying to make it look like you're guilty of something."

"And that's why she searched my place. Jill, if she has the key, all she has to do is try it on Errol's door, and she'll know. Of course, I'll look guilty. I had access to Errol's apartment and kept that from the police."

Helen dropped down to her butt and fell back against the chest of drawers in tears. "Jill, what can I do? I lied to the police!"

"Helen, I know you didn't kill Errol."

"I know you know that, but it looks bad."

"But didn't you have the convention for your candles? That can be your alibi."

"It ended at nine o'clock. After that, I was free. Plus, I took a break in the afternoon to do Errol's session. A few assistants ran the booth while I was gone. If they question them..."

"The police already know you were at his apartment in afternoon. I don't think you have anything to worry about there."

Helen started to pound the floor with her fist. "I had

nothing to do with Errol's death, but the police know I've been in his apartment many times. They know about the payments, and they have threatening emails. And if they find out about the key..."

I sat next to Helen and hugged her. "Don't worry. We'll figure something out. I won't let you be the fall guy."

"How do you plan on doing that?"

"You know who called me earlier? Kelly Walker, Grant's mother."

"What did she want?"

"I don't know. I couldn't talk when she called, but she sounded panicky."

Helen pulled her head away from my shoulder. "Really? I didn't realize you were so close that she would call you with a problem."

"We're not, but..."

"What?"

"We found out Ollie took photos of a woman in your building and some were of her nude."

"Really?"

"That's not all. He passed them on to Grant. I think his mother might have found them and somehow connected it back to Ollie."

"Big deal. Grant and Ollie are teenagers. That's what boys their age think and talk about, right?"

"We found out who that woman was, though. She's a substitute teacher at Ollie and Grant's school."

"Oh, that sort of changes things."

"It does."

"So you think Kelly was calling to chew you out?"

"That's the thing, she didn't sound angry. She sounded...scared."

"People show their anger in different ways. Maybe she just

doesn't like confrontation. Wait, do you think Grant passed those photos on to other students?"

"Ollie said he didn't, but what was stopping him?" I said. "If he did, that could cause a lot of problems."

"If that's what really happened, Ollie has nothing to worry about. Grant is the one who passed them around. Maybe Grant got caught and expelled, and that's why Kelly is calling. You should ask Ollie."

"Maybe..." my voice trailed off.

"Or you could just call Kelly back, and we don't have to sit here overthinking why she called. Call her now. Go on."

Alan had just told me the lawyer advised us not to say anything. Alan even said not to call Kelly back. And here I was, holding my phone, ready to call her.

"What are you waiting for?" Helen asked.

"It's just that Alan spoke to a lawyer today about Ollie."

"Really?" Helen raised an eyebrow. "Sounds like overkill."

"Well, there's one thing I didn't tell you that I'm aware of about Kelly."

"What? Spill the tea." Helen said as she slapped my arm.

"Ollie also took a picture of Kelly and Errol on his balcony."

"Shut up! They were screwing?" Helen rubbed her hands together. "This is getting juicier by the second. I can't believe you were holding back on this."

"I wanted to see what the lawyer said."

"I still don't understand why Alan needed to consult a lawyer. Wait, does Kelly know how Grant found out?"

"I'm not sure, but if she didn't before, she probably knows now. Hence the call."

Helen slapped my arm again. "That's probably it."

"Oww, will you stop hitting me?"

"Sorry. I wonder if the police know she was involved with Errol. She could be a suspect."

"How so?"

"Maybe she also had access to his apartment. Maybe she was there with him Friday night."

"I didn't think of that. And Ollie went camping with Grant and his father for the weekend."

"That means Kelly was all alone. Oh, my God. She totally could have done it. Maybe they had a fight. Maybe Kelly tried to break it off after Grant found out, but something happened and..."

"You think she pushed him over the railing?"

"It could have been an accident. You never know. But I bet she's freaking out because the cops are digging around. What did the lawyer say about that?"

"Alan didn't tell him that. He just told him that Ollie had given Grant the picture. Basically, he advised us not to say anything and let the investigation run its course. The lawyer did say not to assume the police think it's murder. He said it was standard to ask questions and thought they would probably make it a suicide."

"Well, that makes me breathe a little easier. But if they do that and Kelly was involved, she's getting away with murder."

"It's possible. Do you really want to get involved, considering your situation? You should also sit back and see how the investigation plays out."

"You're right. Exposing Kelly would only keep the investigation alive, and I might still get arrested. She could lie, right?"

I thought about the threatening emails and the photos Grant had sent Errol. If the police discovered that Grant sent them, Kelly would have a lot of explaining to do. And she could try and point the finger at me.

"What are you thinking?" Helen asked.

I put my phone away. "We should keep our mouths shut."

Chapter Forty-Two

Alan

MIA WAS CRAVING PIZZA, so I ordered from our local pizzeria. Shortly after, I heard a knock at the front door. *That was quick.* I grabbed my wallet and opened the front door, but instead of finding my pizza delivery, I found two men in suits.

"You must be Mr. Pittman," one of them said.

"That's me. And you are...?

"I'm Detective Sokolov, and this is Detective Bennie. We spoke to your wife this morning."

"She mentioned that. What can I do for you?"

"We had a few more questions. Mind if we come in?"

"Well, Jill's not here right now."

"That's fine. We can ask you the questions."

I stepped aside and pointed them to a small sitting room. "So, what are the questions?"

Detective Bennie placed a photograph on the coffee table. "This is Errol Tiller and Kelly Walker. We spoke to Mrs. Walker today about this photograph. She had already seen it, as her son, Grant, had shown it to her. She said Grant is friends with your son, and she thinks your son took this photo."

"My son's name is Ollie. And yes, we know about this photo

—he took it. He's really into photography and has a pretty decent lens that could capture this. But you should know we've already spoken to him about taking pictures of people in their homes."

"Why was he keeping tabs on Errol Tiller?" Detective Sokolov asked.

"He wasn't. He said he captured this photograph by pure luck. Being the good friend he is, he passed it on to Grant. I'm assuming Grant then confronted his mother. Like I said earlier, Ollie's crazy about photography and is always taking photos. He shouldn't have taken those photos, but there's nothing criminal about that. But like I said, we've spoken to Ollie about respecting people's privacy."

"We're sure you did," Detective Sokolov said. "What do you know about Walker's marital status?"

"The Walkers are married, I thought. We don't really know them like that. Our sons may be best friends, but Jill and I aren't close with Kelly and Kent. I think the Walkers are better equipped to answer that question."

Detective Bennie produced another photo that I recognized right away. It was of Errol and Ms. Martin making a porno.

"While looking through Mr. Tiller's email account, this photo was found in an email sent to Mr. Tiller. Did your son take this photo?"

"It's possible, but what makes you think he did?"

"This photo was in Grant Walker's possession," Detective Bennie said. "It looks like it was shot with the same lens as the photograph of Mr. Tiller and Mrs. Walker on the balcony. You mentioned earlier that your son is crazy about photography and always takes photos."

Detective Bennie put another copy of an email down on the table. "Is this your son's email address?"

I took a look at the sender and recognized it. I also saw who it was sent to: Grant. The photos of Errol Tiller and Ms. Martin were attached.

"Seems like your son has been sharing photos of Mr. Tiller with Grant. Any idea why?"

"None. But I'll have a talk with him. Teenage boys—crazy hormones, right? Do you mind if I ask you a question?"

Detective Sokolov shook his head. "Fire away."

"Why is SFPD so interested in a couple of photos? I mean, photographing people in their apartments isn't anything new. I'm baffled why you would make the trip here to confirm whether my son took the photos or not."

"We need to consider everything when investigating a murder, Mr. Pittman. We believe in being thorough. You have an excellent view of the building Mr. Tiller lives in. Your son might have seen something helpful in the case. Was he home last Friday night?"

"He wasn't. He was away on a weekend camping trip with Grant and Kent."

Detective Bennie put down a few more papers. "These are emails sent to Mr. Tiller from the Walker residence. Threats were made to Mr. Tiller, and your son's photos were used to blackmail him."

I raised my hands up. "Whoa, whoa, whoa. No way Ollie sent these emails. He had no reason to blackmail Mr. Tiller. But you might want to talk to the Walkers."

"We're trying to get everyone's side of the story."

"Wait, did the Walkers suggest Ollie was responsible for these emails?"

"Was he?" Detective Sokolov asked. "They were sent a few weeks ago."

"Look, this is becoming a much more formal conversation than I anticipated. If you want to continue this conversation, we can do that with my lawyer present."

"That's fine, because we want to ask Ollie some questions directly. Your wife still has my card, but here's another one. She was supposed to bring your daughter in for questioning today, but I didn't hear back from her. We also want to hear about what happened while Mia interned at Tiller & Associates. You're aware of the sexual harassment report she filed against Mr. Tiller, right?"

"My wife told me, yes. When she gets back, I'll talk to her, and we'll call back with the day and time we can come in."

"We appreciate your cooperation, Mr. Pittman."

Chapter Forty-Three

Alan

TRUTH BE TOLD, I was a little worried about this most recent visit from the detectives. That was two in the same day. In the back of my mind, I always suspected the police would find those emails. It was standard procedure to look through email, phone records, and social media for clues.

According to Larry, Ollie hadn't done anything wrong. The police would have to provide evidence showing that Ollie conspired with Grant to send those emails with the intent to blackmail Errol. So far, it appeared Grant had worked alone. Of course, I was concerned—Ollie's my son—but I also knew Larry was a great attorney. I grabbed my cell to update him.

"Alan, is there a new development?" Larry asked.

"I just spoke with the same detectives who questioned Jill this morning. They found the emails that Grant sent to Errol. They wanted to know if Ollie was involved. Really, they want to question him."

"And how did you answer?"

"I told them that Ollie had taken the pictures, which they already knew because shortly after, they produced an email of Ollie sending those pictures to Grant. Sneaky guys."

"Yeah, they like to do that. Admitting Ollie took the photos and sent them to Grant is fine. Were there any instructions in the email, or suggestions on what to do with them?"

"None."

"Perfect."

"They did mention they would still like to question Ollie. He wasn't home while they were here. Also, Jill decided not to take Mia in for questioning today, so that's two outstanding requests from the police to interview our kids."

"It may sound frightening, but it's just questions. You'll need to officially retain me if I'm going to be a part of the questioning."

"That's fine. Thanks, Larry."

The pizza delivery showed up right after I ended the call.

"Mia," I called out. "Pizza's here."

She came down in a hurry, rubbing her hands together. "I'm so starved," she said.

"The box on top is pepperoni, and the one on the bottom is veggie," I said before taking a bite of my slice.

We both stood next to the kitchen island, eating quietly.

"Was someone here? I thought I heard someone," she managed in between chews.

"A couple of detectives stopped by with questions. They found the emails that Grant had sent to Errol. And they also have the emails Ollie sent to Grant with the photos attached."

"Is Ollie in trouble now?"

"No, because Ollie did nothing wrong. It's not against the law to photograph someone in their home, so long as you're not on their property while you do it."

"Really?"

"That's why the paparazzi can get away with it."

"Oh yeah, I guess so."

"Plus, I saw the email that Ollie sent to Grant. He didn't tell Grant to send the photos to Errol."

"Well, that's good. So what will happen now?"

"Both you and your brother will need to go in to the police station and answer a few questions. It's nothing to worry about. I have a lawyer who tells me this is all standard procedure."

"When do we need to do this?"

"As soon as your mother gets home, we'll figure out a game plan."

Just then, the front door burst open, and in walked Ollie. "Is that pizza I smell?"

"Yeah, there's pepperoni and veggie," I said.

"Awesome, I'm starved," he said as he grabbed a slice and shoved half of it into his mouth. "Mmmm, this is so good."

Mia brushed off her hands. "Thanks for the pizza, Dad."

"The police were here again," I said once Mia had left. "You're not in trouble, Ollie. I'm just cluing you in."

"What did they want?"

"They found the emails Grant sent to Errol with the pictures you took."

"They know I took them?"

"Yes, and it's fine, because what you did isn't illegal. What Grant did could have implications; mainly, it could be considered blackmail. The police will want to ask you a few questions, but it's nothing to worry about. They'll want to confirm what they already know and hear directly from you that you were not involved with Grant's plan to threaten Errol."

"I wasn't."

"I know, buddy."

"I feel bad, though. Grant's my best friend."

"I know, but he also did something he shouldn't have. I understand why he did it. He was angry with his mother and lashed out at Errol. I'm sure the police will see it that way, as well."

"I hope so. Grant really is a great guy."

"Ollie, are there any other photos I need to know about, or emails, or anything involving Errol? Now is the time to tell me."

"That's it, Dad. I swear."

"Okay, because if there is, I need to tell the lawyer."

"We have a lawyer? I thought you said we have nothing to worry about."

"We don't. I have a lawyer for precautions and to keep it so we have nothing to worry about. He knows everything that's happened so far, and he doesn't think you did anything wrong or have anything to worry about."

"That's good to know."

"Ollie... out of curiosity, do you know if the Walkers are having problems with their marriage?"

"You mean, does Mr. Walker know about the affair? According to Grant, he has no clue. That's why Grant hated Mr. Tiller. He couldn't stand seeing his dad say 'hi' to him in the lobby. But ever since Mr. Tiller died, Grant said everything is great in his family. I mean, things are back to normal with him and his mom. For a while, he was super angry at her. It even started to affect our friendship."

"Yeah, I can see how that could happen."

"So, is Grant in trouble?"

"I don't know. The police might say those emails made Errol commit suicide, but I read them. I can't see how they could have driven him to that point. Errol might have had many problems in his life already and decided to end them. This whole scandal with Grant's mother might have had no role in his decision. There's no proof that it did."

"Okay. Thanks, Dad—you know, for being cool. Mom's a little freaked out, but you aren't."

"I'm just as concerned as your mother. We just express ourselves differently. She loves and supports you. In fact, what you think is freaking out is her worrying about you. She doesn't want to see you get into trouble. And that's the truth."

Chapter Forty-Four

Kelly

WAITING for Grant to come home from school had my mind racing and conjuring up scenarios and possibilities it had no reason to. I needed answers, and they could only come from Grant. He hadn't answered my messages or phone calls, which drove me nuts.

When he finally walked through the front door, it took everything I had not to fire off a million questions, one after the other. I was so angry with him—for ignoring me, for sending those emails and photos to Errol. And the worst part was, I knew why he had done it. It was because of me. I drove him to do that. It reminded me how selfish I was to think my actions would affect only me.

But the worst of it all was the list. It read like a manifesto. I kept telling myself that there had to be a reasonable explanation. At least, that's what I wanted to believe.

At the same time, I couldn't help but think: Maybe there were other things he did that I, or the police, were unaware of. Perhaps a combination of different threats from him made Errol commit suicide.

"Grant, where have you been? I've been trying to reach you all afternoon."

"I'm sorry, Mom. I was in a photography club meeting."

"Why didn't you just text me that?"

He shrugged. "What's wrong?"

"Have a seat. We need to talk."

Grant slipped off his backpack and sat on a chair next to me.

"The police were here today."

"Why?"

"Grant, they know about the emails you sent to Errol."

Grant looked away from me.

"They know about the photos and the threats you made. I know this is my fault; I realize you did this because of me. But why would you think doing something like that would help the situation?"

"I didn't do anything wrong. You did. You cheated on Dad."

"And I don't deny it. But I told you I would handle things. I told you I would end it with him immediately. And I did."

"So what?" he snapped back as he eyed me.

"'So what?' Those emails constitute blackmail, Grant. You can get into trouble for that."

Grant looked away again, not saying anything.

I held up the list. "I also found this in your room. I need you to explain this."

Grant looked at the paper. "It's nothing, Mom. I was angry. I learned in school that if you write stuff down, it helps your mental health. That's all it is."

"Oh, don't give me that."

"It's true. I learned it."

"Okay, then why is Ollie's name on the paper? Was this his idea?"

"No, Mom. In this world, or place, or whatever you want to call it, I felt like I needed a partner. He's my best friend so he's there for support. I swear, Mom. I wasn't serious about doing any of that stuff."

I took a brief moment to think about everything Grant had said, knowing full well we wouldn't even be having this conversation if I hadn't strayed. "Okay, I believe you."

"Do you? Because it sounds like you think I had something to do with Mr. Tiller's death."

"I know you didn't, because you were away camping. I just want to make sure I understand the complete picture in case the police come back. They don't care if you're angry or if it was a joke. They see threats, and now there's a dead man."

"I didn't kill him."

"I know, and we need to make sure the police understand that, as well. I already told them I would bring you to the station."

"What? Why?"

"Because, Grant, we need to make sure they understand the reason behind the emails. It will help if they hear it from you. I've already told them you were angry with me, and that's why you did what you did."

"Whatever."

"Also, I'm asking that you not mention this to your father. I've learned from my mistake, and I hope you can forgive me one day. I love you very much, Grant. I hope you know that."

"I know, Mom."

I brushed Grant's hair out of his eyes before moving on to my last line of questioning.

"Grant, does Ollie know what you did?"

"Yeah, but he didn't have anything to do with the emails."

"Do you think he told his parents?"

"They know he took the photos. They found them. And they know he sent them to me."

Great. Now I have the Pittmans to deal with as well.

"What about the emails to Errol?"

"I'm not sure."

"I'm guessing they know everything. If Ollie weren't so much of a Peeping Tom, we wouldn't be in this mess right now."

"Mom, we're in this mess because of you. You were the one having an affair with Mr. Tiller."

Just then, a noise off to the side caught my attention. Standing in the open front door was Kent, with a dumbfounded look on his face.

"Grant, what did you just say?"

"Kent, I can explain," I said.

"Kelly, were you having an affair with Errol Tiller?"

"It's not like that."

He shut the door behind him. "Well, Grant seems to think you were. What other reason would he have to say it?"

"Grant, can you excuse yourself while your dad and I talk, please?"

"No, Grant. Stay right there. I want to hear what else he has to say about Errol and you."

"Kent, please."

"I can't take it anymore!" Grant shouted as he threw up his hands.

"Grant, where are you going?" I asked.

"Grant, sit back down," Kent said, grabbing his arm.

Grant shook himself loose, pushed past Kent, and left the apartment. "You guys figure it out!" he shouted from the hall.

Chapter Forty-Five

Jill

The way Helen and I had left things was that she would take the same approach that Alan and I were taking. She'd keep her mouth shut and see how the investigation progressed. I advised her not to approach Peggy or any staff member about the key. Helen could now deny having had it. And if any of them (meaning Peggy) fought her on that, they'd have to admit to entering Helen's apartment without her permission and stealing from her. She couldn't tell the police, because that would also incriminate her.

Honestly, it seemed like Helen and Grant were in the same situation. Both had lashed out at Errol recently because of something he did. That, to me, didn't paint them as opportunists; it made Errol look like a scumbag. If one person is angry with you, they might be the problem. But if multiple people around you are angry with you, you need to look inside and see if you're the problem. At least, that's how I saw it.

I still felt a little guilty for keeping things from Helen.

On my way out of the building, I spotted Grant sitting on the curb with his head hanging between his legs.

"Hi, Grant," I said as I approached him from behind.

He didn't acknowledge my salutation, so I called his name once more and got the same reaction.

"Grant. It's me, Mrs. Pittman."

"Oh, hi," he said in a soft voice.

I took a seat next to him. "Grant, do you want to tell me what happened?"

"No, that's okay."

I saw a teardrop hit the pavement. "Grant, are your parents home?"

"Yeah."

I knew right then what must have happened. Kelly Walker's secret was out—and probably Grant's—and now his parents were arguing. The sun would go down soon, and I didn't feel like leaving Grant to sit outside alone. "Tell you what. Why don't you come and have dinner at my house? You can hang out with Ollie."

"Okay."

I didn't bother to ask questions on the drive back. It wasn't any of my business. Once we were inside my home, Grant headed upstairs to Ollie's room. Alan spied us from the kitchen, so I went to talk to him.

"What's Grant doing here?" he asked.

"I passed him on the way out of Helen's building. He was sitting on the curb, crying. I think his parents were arguing."

Alan nodded. "So, Kent knows. Even I wouldn't want to be there. It's good that you came out when you did. Did you let them know Grant is over here?"

"I sent Kelly a message."

"Good. Anything new with Helen? How's the candle business?"

It dawned on me that, with all that had been happening with Ollie and Mia and the police, I still hadn't told Alan about

Helen's involvement. At first, I hadn't planned to, but now I felt I had to.

"Uh, actually, there's something I need to tell you about Helen."

I walked Alan through everything Helen had told me, from her dominatrix business, to the threats she sent Errol, to the key to his apartment.

"Jill, didn't you think this was important to tell me?"

"I'm telling you now."

Alan ran his hand through his hair. I knew he was angry. This was a big deal, but it hadn't necessarily seemed that way when Helen first confided in me.

"So she thinks Peggy snuck into her apartment and stole the key?"

"Yes."

"What the hell does Peggy have to do with any of this? It's like Errol had his slimy tentacles wrapped around everyone. You know, there's a chance Helen's more involved than she's letting on. With a key, it means she had access. She could have visited Errol late that night."

"Helen has absolutely nothing to do with Errol's death. I know her."

"Are you sure?"

"Alan!"

"Okay, okay. Well, this helps take the spotlight further off of Ollie. Did she say how the police responded to this information?"

"They only know about her financial arrangement with Errol and the emails she sent. They don't know about the key."

"She lied about the key?"

"She forgot she had it."

"How convenient."

"Oh, please, Alan. Helen's not a threat to us—unlike Kelly and Grant."

"You're right about that, but boy, isn't this the mother of all shitstorms. Can you imagine all these things coming out, and you've been assigned to this investigation?"

"I don't need to imagine it. I'm living it."

"Well, I'll add to this quagmire. The cops stopped by while you were over at Helen's. They found the threatening emails Grant had sent to Errol, which we assumed they would. They also had the photos and wanted to know if they came from Ollie."

"What did you tell them?"

"I told them that Ollie had taken those pictures, which isn't illegal, and that he probably sent them to Grant. But I assured them that Ollie had nothing to do with the threatening emails sent to Errol."

"Why did you admit to that?"

"They had spoken to Kelly earlier in the day, and she must have pointed them to Ollie. It didn't make sense to try and cover it up. If they didn't have solid proof already, they would have come up with it pretty quickly."

"So now they know it started with Ollie and ended with Grant," I said.

"Well, that's a simplistic explanation of it, yes. Look, Ollie's not in trouble. As soon as those detectives left, I filled Larry in. He still stands by what he said earlier. The cops still want to speak to Mia and Ollie. Larry said it's par for the course, and we don't need to worry. But I have retained him, and he'll be in the meeting looking out for our interests. Honestly, as guilty as Grant looks, he wasn't around when Tiller went over that railing, and neither was Ollie. And I hate to say it, but...Helen was. And she had a key."

"Stop it with the Helen accusations. She didn't do it."

213

But Alan's words struck a chord with me. I mean, how well did I really know Helen? She did lie about being a dominatrix, and she never went into detail about her life back in New York, always telling me she didn't want to bore me with those details. What if I hadn't come close to scratching the surface of who she was?

"Could this be why Kelly called earlier? To warn me?"

"Or to pick your brain for ammunition," Alan said. "This is why Larry doesn't want us speaking to anyone. Our words can be used against us. And at the rate things are progressing, there could be more revelations. What's Peggy's involvement? It has to be big for her to break into Helen's apartment."

I shrugged.

"That's why we can't say anything. We'll set up an appointment tomorrow for the kids to be questioned, and then we'll have done our part."

Chapter Forty-Six

Ollie

THE SECOND GRANT walked into my bedroom, I knew something was messed up.

"What happened?" I asked as I spun my chair around.

"Everything is totally screwed again." He flopped onto my bed.

"What do you mean? I thought everything was better now."

"It was, but the cops came by my house today. They found my emails to Mr. Tiller and showed them to my mom."

"Was she pissed?"

"She wasn't happy. So I started telling her what I did, and then we started to argue, and then the next thing I knew, I yelled out that it was her fault, and she shouldn't have been having an affair with Mr. Tiller. My dad walked in right when I said that."

"No way. That's insane."

"I know, right? So they started arguing, and I bailed because I couldn't take it. Your mom saw me outside and brought me here."

"I'm glad she did. You're better off here. Your parents need to figure that stuff out."

"There's more. She found the kill list we made."

"Shit. What did she say?"

"She wanted to know why I made it. I told her I was angry and that it was something I learned in school to help with my mental health. Don't worry, she believed me. She thinks I wrote it all and you were on it for moral support, fictionally. Don't stress."

"Are you sure?"

"Why are you acting like this? You said you would help do whatever we needed to make Mr. Tiller pay."

"I know, but..."

"Come on, Ollie. You hated Mr. Tiller, too, especially after you found out he'd been hooking up with Ms. Martin."

After seeing how the affair affected Grant, sure, I was pissed off at the guy. He was a prick for pursuing Grant's mom. He knew she was married. That dude could have gotten any number of women in the city; why pick Mrs. Walker?

"What do you think will happen now?" I asked.

"Nothing," Grant said. "We have rock-solid alibis. Even that worked out in our favor. I think the police will eventually rule it a suicide."

"Yeah, I think so, too. I have to talk to the police tomorrow."

"About what? The photos?" Grant asked.

"Yeah, and probably the email."

"My mom said they wanted to talk to me, too."

"Don't worry. So long as we both stick to our story, we should be fine."

I held out my hand, and Grant gave it a fist bump.

"Hey, is Ms. Martin home?"

"I don't know. Let's check." I popped out of my chair and grabbed my camera.

"Nah, her lights are off," I said, looking through the viewfinder. "Actually, she's been out a lot lately."

"Let me see," Grant said.

I held the camera in place until he took it from me.

"I wonder if her gig is over at school or if she's just taking a break," he said as he took a look.

"I'm not sure." I sat back down on the bed. "I feel bad using her photos to get back at Mr. Tiller."

"Yeah, same here. She's a nice lady, but I don't think it bothers her. She's making pornos."

"I bet she has an OF account." He put my camera down and quickly grabbed his phone.

"Yeah, let's try and find it," I said.

We spent the next ten minutes using different name combinations (and even tried looking for teacher characters) but came up empty.

"This is impossible," I said.

"I'm sure she's using an alias that's not even close to her real name," Grant said.

"Yeah, and plus, she wears a mask. I guess it's good that we didn't do anything more with those photos. It could have screwed up her teaching gig."

"Do you think the police will think Ms. Martin had something to do with Mr. Tiller's death?" Grant asked. "You know, because of the photos."

I thought about his question. "Maybe, if Mr. Tiller and Ms. Martin had problems with the videos."

Grant rubbed his belly. "I can't wait for dinner. Your mom said she's making spaghetti."

"Sweet. You should just crash here. That way, we can play video games the rest of the night."

"Sounds like an awesome plan."

Chapter Forty-Seven

Jill

THE FOLLOWING DAY, we were all set to take Ollie and Mia to the police station to answer questions. Rather than wait all day for the kids to finish school, I scheduled the meeting for that morning. Larry, our lawyer, was meeting us there.

Mia, Ollie, and Grant were sitting at the kitchen island finishing their breakfast. They all seemed to be in a good mood, especially Grant. Spending the night at our place had helped, apparently. I hadn't told Mia and Ollie about the appointment at the police station; I wanted to wait until after I dropped Grant off.

"Hey Grant, are you about ready? Your mom is expecting you."

"Yeah, sure, Mrs. Pittman," he said. Then, turning to Ollie, "See you in school." They bumped fists.

The drive to Grant's building only took five minutes, enough time for him to thank me for letting him spend the night and eat dinner at our house.

"Grant, you know you're always welcome." I pulled the car up to the curb in front of his building.

"Have a great day, Mrs. Pittman," he said as he climbed out.

I looked beyond Grant into the lobby but didn't see Kelly.

Ollie was still sitting in the kitchen when I returned home. "Where's your sister?"

"She wanted to change her outfit again. She's crazy."

"Mia, could you come down here?" I called out.

A few minutes later, she came down wearing the same outfit.

Teenage girls: always changing their minds.

"Listen, you both have appointments to speak to the police this morning."

"Right now?" Mia looked like she'd just seen a ghost.

"It's nothing to worry about, Mia. They just want to ask about your time working at Tiller & Associates."

We hadn't told Ollie about what had happened to Mia. It was a private matter for her. If she wanted to tell him, she could.

"Ollie, you already know what they want to talk about. You just need to tell them what you know, the same way you told your father and me."

"Okay. Is Dad coming with us?" Ollie asked.

"I am," Alan said as he appeared from around the corner.

The Central Police Station, in North Beach, wasn't more than a ten-minute drive from the house. We left our car in the parking structure near the station and walked inside. Alan greeted Larry with a handshake.

"Larry, this is my wife, Jill, and our kids, Mia and Ollie."

"Nice to meet you all. Everything is all set up. Shall we get started?"

A few moments later, Detective Sokolov appeared and escorted us to the interview rooms. They had Mia wait in one; I stayed with her. Alan and Ollie were taken into another room.

"You can keep them separated, but you will only speak to them one at a time and while I'm present," Larry said. "Are we in agreement?"

"Sure thing," Detective Sokolov said. "Let's start with Ollie."

Mia and I waited in the interview room while Ollie was questioned.

"Do you think Ollie will be okay?" Mia asked quietly.

"I do." I reached out and squeezed my daughter's hand. "From what I've been told, they want to ask him the same questions they asked your father and me. We already told them everything. This is more like the police wanting to hear it from Ollie. He's got nothing to worry about."

"Good. I'm still confused about why they need to talk to me. They already know what happened from the report."

"I think it's to make sure that what you have to say matches the report. But you're right, I'm not sure how relevant it is. Were there complaints from other women about Errol?"

"I'm not sure. I didn't ask, and they didn't say. But I got the feeling from the HR director that it wasn't the first case."

"What made you think that?"

"She had this look on her face when I told her. You know, like, 'Really, this again?' It wasn't in a mocking way. She genuinely cared for my safety and took the complaint seriously. I never felt like they were brushing me off, but I still knew nothing would come of it."

"But you filed it, and that's important. Because now it's been established, and if it happened before, it paints a picture."

"Yeah, I never had any contact with Mr. Tiller after that. So maybe he did do it in the past, and the only way they could handle it was by separating him from the person who filed the complaint, because he's the owner."

"Maybe."

About twenty minutes had passed before the door to our room opened. In walked the two detectives, followed by Larry.

"Jill, Alan and Ollie are waiting in the other room. Everything went fine," Larry said, giving me a reassuring smile.

"Hi, Mia. I'm Detective Sokolov, and this is Detective Bennie. We've already read the complaint you filed at Tiller & Associates, so we only have a few follow-up questions."

"Okay," she said.

"While in Mr. Tiller's presence, did you notice any signs of him being under the influence of drugs or alcohol?"

"You mean, like, acting like he was drunk?"

"Yes, or it could be much more subtle, like losing his balance, or slurring a word, or even hyperactivity—acting like he had an unusually high amount of energy."

"Well...once I had to deliver something to him in his office, and when he spoke to me, I could smell alcohol on his breath. It was 9:30 in the morning. He didn't look or act drunk. I just smelled it."

"Did he ever tell you about his personal life, like problems he might have been having or things happening in his life? Maybe a party or an outing?"

"No, nothing like that." Mia shook her head. "He was always asking me questions about my life, though."

"Were any of those questions about what you did after school or at night?"

"Yeah. He'd want to know if I always went straight home after school or had some school activity to go to."

"I'm sorry, detectives, but what does this have to do with Mr. Tiller's death?" Larry asked.

"While looking through Mr. Tiller's computer, we found images of women—girls—who appeared to be minors. As you know, Mr. Tiller owns a telescope. Apparently, he was using it to look into people's homes."

"Ewww," Mia said. "You think he spied on me?"

"We didn't find any pictures of you, but it's possible. Your home address would be in your employment files."

"What a bastard!" I said.

"Mia, why didn't you tell your parents about Mr. Tiller's behavior?"

"I didn't want to worry them."

"It wasn't because you enjoyed the attention?"

"Detective, my daughter is the victim here. How dare you insinuate she was 'asking for it'?" I said.

"Mr. Tiller is a good-looking, charming man, not to mention wealthy," he continued, keeping his focus on Mia as if I had never objected.

"This is absurd," I said.

Detective Bennie placed a few pieces of paper on the table. "These screen captures were taken from the security cameras in Mr. Tiller's office."

I leaned forward to take a closer look and saw Mia talking to Mr. Tiller while he sat behind his desk. In one photo, she appeared to be laughing. In another, she struck a seductive pose. I couldn't believe my eyes. I picked them up and looked at them carefully. Mia didn't look frightened of Mr. Tiller, or even annoyed. She was smiling and giggling. My stomach dropped. I couldn't believe what I was looking at. Surely, these photos were doctored. This couldn't be my teenage daughter flirting with her much older boss.

"Mom, it's not what you think," Mia said.

"Mia..." I shook my head. I didn't know what to say.

"You can understand why we had our questions," Detective Sokolov said.

"Mom, Mr. Tiller asked about TikTok dances. That's all this is. It's not what it seems. All I did was show him the dance. That's all. And this was before he started asking creepy questions."

Larry leaned over and took the photos from my hand.

"It's just that we have evidence of your son photographing Mr. Tiller," Detective Sokolov said. "Those photographs were used to threaten Mr. Tiller. And now we have these photos of your daughter flirting with him."

"Excuse me, detectives," Larry interrupted. "Is there audio attached to this security footage?"

"No, there's no audio," Detective Bennie said.

"So you have no proof of what was said during this exchange between Mia Pittman and Errol Tiller."

"And that's why we're asking Mia," Detective Bennie said.

"Mia has already answered that question. What you're doing now is taking things out of context. Are there more questions to be asked? If not, this meeting is over."

"That's all for now," Detective Sokolov said. "We apologize, Mrs. Pittman, if we upset you. We're only trying to figure out what happened."

"Come on, Mia. Let's go."

Alan and Ollie were waiting in the hallway when we stepped out of the interview room.

"How did it go?" Alan asked.

My chest had tightened, and my breathing was labored.

"Jill, is something wrong?"

"Can we talk about it outside?"

"Yeah, sure."

Just then, the Walkers appeared at the other end of the hall. Grant was with them.

"Excuse us," Detective Sokolov said as he and his partner brushed past us to greet the Walkers.

"I know how to get out of here," Larry said. "Follow me."

I couldn't get out of that place fast enough. Once we were outside, on the sidewalk, I drew a deep breath.

"That's it, Jill. Just breathe," Alan said as he comforted me. "What happened in there, Larry?"

"The police were insinuating that Mia made a false sexual harassment claim."

"Sexual harassment?" Ollie said. "Mr. Tiller did that to you?"

"Dad, I didn't lie!" Mia said. "It's true what he did. The photos they had were of me doing a TikTok dance."

I stood there listening to the conversation, still in disbelief that what should have been a simple rehash of the questions Alan and I had already answered had turned into an interrogation, making us look like we were covering something up.

"Look, don't worry. They're just trying to see if they can trip you up," Larry said. "They don't have anything, and that's why they pulled that bull back there."

"Will they do the same to the Walkers?" I asked.

"Who are the Walkers?" Larry asked.

"That couple that was in the hallway. Their son is Grant, Ollie's friend," Alan said.

"Ah, okay. I understand. Because they're questioning the Walkers, my advice is that you not have any contact with them."

"You mean I can't talk to my friend?" Ollie asked.

"For now, you should take a break," Larry said before turning back to Alan. "Once we know how the investigation is settled, we can reevaluate your family's relationship with the Walkers."

Chapter Forty-Eight

Kelly

It was a little awkward seeing the Pittmans at the police station. Clearly, they had just gotten done giving statements. Did they blame Grant for everything?

"It looks like the Pittmans retained a lawyer," I said to Kent. "Maybe we should think about getting one."

"I'll look into it."

It didn't help that Kent and I also had to deal with my infidelity. I was sure it was hard for him to even be around me at the moment, but the meeting with the police was unavoidable. I told him he didn't need to come, but he insisted on being present.

"We appreciate you coming in. You must be Mr. Walker," the detective said, holding out a hand to Kent. "I'm Detective Sokolov, and this is Detective Bennie. We're investigating Errol Tiller's death. We just have a few questions for your son. It shouldn't take long."

He led us into an interview room, and we sat at a small table.

"Were you taking statements from the Pittmans?" I asked.

"I'm sorry, but we can't discuss the investigation with you,"

Detective Sokolov said before turning his attention to my son. "Grant, there's no need to be afraid. We're just talking here."

"Do we need a lawyer?" I asked.

"You're well within your rights to retain counsel, but we're just having a simple conversation here."

"Mom, it's fine," Grant said. "I don't have a problem answering their questions."

I watched Detective Bennie spread out copies of the emails that Grant had sent to Errol.

"Grant, did you send these emails to Mr. Tiller?"

Grant took a closer look. "I did. I wanted him to leave my mom alone. I was angry at him for causing problems in my family."

"Did Mr. Tiller ever respond to you?"

"No, because he didn't know I sent the emails. I created an email account just for him, under a fake name."

"Well, he might have suspected it was someone from your family, since the picture was of him and your mother."

"I guess."

"So, no contact at all? Not even a suspicious look in the lobby?"

"No."

"Grant, how did finding out about Mr. Tiller's death make you feel?"

"Happy. I wouldn't have to worry about him making trouble in my family again."

"Was that the plan? To make him disappear?"

"What plan?" Grant asked.

"Did you and your best friend, Ollie Pittman, want to do something to Mr. Tiller? Ollie took the pictures of Mr. Tiller and gave them to you. You two were working together."

"Grant, not another word," Kent said. "Detectives, we need to end this meeting. We can continue it once we have a lawyer."

Detective Sokolov held up his hands. "Completely understand. Just let us know when you want to reschedule. Grant's a minor, so we get it. But your wife—we had some questions for her, as well."

"What questions?" I asked. "I told you everything I know."

"Detectives," Kent said, raising his voice. "I said this meeting is over."

Kent stood up and motioned for us to leave the room.

"Kent, I'd like to stay and talk to them. You and Grant can wait out in the hall. I have nothing to hide, because no one in this family had anything to do with Errol falling over his railing."

"Kelly, I don't think it's a good idea."

"It's fine. Kent, please."

Once Kent and Grant were out of the room, I turned back to the detectives. "Ask your questions."

"Thank you, Mrs. Walker. The DNA sample you voluntarily provided for us matches DNA we found in Mr. Tiller's apartment," Detective Sokolov said. "Primarily the samples found on his bedsheets. Did you visit Mr. Tiller Friday night?"

"I did. I didn't mention it before because I was embarrassed, and I was afraid my husband would find out. I'd already told Grant I had broken it off with Errol."

"But you didn't?"

"I did, but he kept calling me to meet him. He finally told me if I didn't come to him one last time, he would tell my husband. And that's why I visited him on Friday."

"Where was your family?"

"Grant was away on a camping trip with my husband and Ollie Pittman."

"Was it late when you visited Mr. Tiller?"

"I would say I went up to his apartment at around midnight.

227

I was there for an hour. And when I left, he was very much alive —high on cocaine, but alive."

"Did you do cocaine while you were there?"

"No, I never touched that stuff. I didn't go up there to party. I went up there to have sex with him one last time, and that's it."

"And you were there for an hour? That's some pretty good closure."

"The cocaine made it difficult for him to finish. Trust me, none of it was exciting for me."

Detective Sokolov looked at his partner. "Do you recall if CSI logged a used condom or wrapper?"

"I don't believe they did," Detective Bennie said.

"The condom and wrapper was flushed," I said.

I opened up my purse and pulled out the burner phone I had used to communicate with Errol. "You can see the text messages we exchanged that night. It'll validate everything I said to you."

Detective Sokolov read the messages. "Can we keep this?"

"Sure, I don't need it anymore. ...Are you going to tell my husband what we just discussed?"

"At the moment, I don't see any reason to do so," Sokolov said.

"I'd appreciate it if it stayed that way."

"We'll do our best, but you must understand, our objective is finding out the truth about Mr. Tiller's death. We have no interest in your marriage. One last question: Did you see Mr. Tiller's dog when you visited him?"

"I don't recall seeing it, but it's not a big dog. It could have been sleeping in another room."

"Thank you for sticking around. We appreciate your cooperation, Mrs. Walker."

Chapter Forty-Nine

Jill

ON THE WAY to dropping the kids off at school, Alan reiterated the importance of listening to what the lawyer said: Don't talk to anybody, including the Walkers. Mia didn't have a problem with the directive. Ollie was a totally different story.

"Are you telling me I can't be friends with Grant?" Ollie asked. "It's not like I can 'unfriend' him like that." Ollie snapped his fingers.

"Are you dense, Ollie?" Mia asked. "Mom and Dad aren't asking you to kick him out of your life. All they're saying is to take a break."

"Easy for you to say. You still get to talk to all of your friends."

"Mia's right, Ollie," I said. "You're just taking a break. That's all. Once this investigation blows over, everything can return to normal."

"But—"

"Listen to your mother, Ollie," Alan said. "We're not playing around here."

Alan brought the car to a stop next to the curb.

"Ollie, stay put. You're coming home with us."

Ty Hutchinson

"Bye," Mia said as she closed the door and headed into the school building.

"Why can't I go to school?"

"Because I said so."

"Because you think I'll talk to Grant, right? What if we have an assignment we have to work on together? Can I talk to him then? Or what about the photography club? Is it okay to talk to him there? What are the dos and don'ts here? Let's break it down."

"Ollie, this isn't a negotiation. This is me telling you how it's going to be."

Ollie and Alan continued to trade barbs all the way back home, until Alan finally lost it.

"Ollie, if I find out you spoke to Grant, even a single text or a single phone call—if you so much as send him a smoke signal—this unfriending will be permanent, and you'll enjoy the solitude of your room every day after school until you're eighteen."

Ollie mumbled something as he headed into the house.

"What did you say?" Alan asked.

"I said it's unfair!"

"You think *this* is unfair? No, I don't think you understand what 'unfair' is." Alan grabbed Ollie by his arm and took his phone from him.

"Hey! You can't take that."

"I just did."

"But it's mine."

"I bought it, so it's mine. I only lent it to you."

Alan then wrangled Ollie's backpack off of him and pulled out his laptop.

"Taking this back, too."

"What are you doing?"

"I'm showing you what 'unfair' really is."

230

Alan then headed upstairs to Ollie's bedroom and rounded up all of his photography equipment.

"Okay, I think that's pretty unfair," he said. "I hope this demonstration between fair and unfair is clear enough for you. Now go to your room and stay there."

Ollie stomped up the stairs and slammed his bedroom door. I thought for a second Alan would go after him, but he just sat on a stool in the kitchen.

"Don't you think you're being a little harsh?" I said.

"Jill, Ollie needs to understand this isn't a game. There could be real repercussions, and you and I cannot protect him from them. I mean, this pertains to everything, not just this situation. That kid hasn't taken anything we said seriously over the last few days."

"I won't argue with that."

"All he's done is lie or withhold information from us."

"I've never seen you this way. Usually, I'm the one who's the bad cop around here."

"Well, it's time I shoulder some of that responsibility. I don't want this situation spinning out of control."

Alan grabbed a bottle of water from the fridge. Seeing him take charge like that in the heat of the moment made me feel supported in parenting. Alan had never really been the disciplinarian in the family, so to see him step up—with no prodding from me—was refreshing. It also made my heart flutter a bit.

"What?" he asked, pulling the bottle away from his lips after taking a swig. "Why are you smiling at me like that?"

"Well, it's just that you also bought my phone for me. Are you taking it away?" I asked playfully.

Alan chuckled. "Tell you what. Be a bad girl later tonight, and I'll let you keep it."

Chapter Fifty

Nicole Martin

I HAD JUST FINISHED VACUUMING my apartment when I heard a knock at the door. I opened it and found two men in suits. I didn't know either of them.

"Ms. Nicole Martin?"

"Yes, that's me."

"I'm Detective Sokolov, and this is my partner, Detective Bennie. We're with the San Francisco Police." The detective flashed a badge. "Do you have a moment to answer a few questions for us?"

"About what?"

"We're investigating the death of Errol Tiller. It's our understanding that you knew him."

"Oh. Yes, I did. Come inside." I held open the door and motioned the pair toward the couch. "How did you learn about my relationship with Errol? And are you aware of the type of relationship we had?"

"We only know you had a relationship with Mr. Tiller."

"I see."

"Ms. Martin, when was the last time you saw Mr. Tiller in person?"

"Last week, here in my apartment. The nature of that visit was purely business. We filmed an erotic video for my website."

"And what website is that?"

"I have an account on OnlyFans. I'm not ashamed of what I do. I'm proud of my work and the following I've built up."

I opened my laptop and navigated to my page on OF. "Here, I'm Holly Robinson. My character is a strict teacher who gives out lessons. That's Errol right there." I pointed to a masked man in a video thumbnail. "Do you want to see the video?"

"Does he keep his face covered the entire time?"

"He does. So do I. When I'm not doing this, I'm a substitute teacher. I need to protect my identity. Normally I wouldn't name him, but considering the situation..."

"How did you and Mr. Tiller come to have this relationship?"

"It started off as a one-night stand. He wanted seconds, and I didn't. But he had a large one and a great body, so I offered him work with me. It was strictly business between us, or at least it was for me. I have copies of contracts signed by Errol that give me control over the content. I would pay him two thousand dollars per video. He's not entitled to anything else. But the videos took off from the start, and it really boosted my money. Errol wanted a bigger cut of the profits, but I declined. He threatened to out me and hurt my teaching job. I ended my relationship with him right then and there. Here's the email. I saved it."

I turned the laptop a bit so they could read it.

"I've since replaced him with other actors," I said.

"How many videos did you two make?" Detective Sokolov asked.

"Just three. I have zero tolerance for that bullshit he tried to pull."

"Did he try to contact you after you ended the relationship?"

"Yup, but I just kept blocking him wherever I could."

"This video looks like it was filmed here. Did you ever go to his apartment?"

"Never. The one-night stand and the filming all happened here. Look, I am a businesswoman, and I do very well with my OF account. In fact, I've recently given up teaching to pursue this full time. I hired Errol to make videos with me. Nothing more."

"Did Mr. Tiller discuss personal information with you? Other women he was seeing?"

"You mean Kelly Walker. Yeah, he mentioned her. He didn't go into detail, but I figured they were more than coffee buddies. He complained about her pulling back, a.k.a. breaking it off. I didn't ask for details of the relationship. I just listened to him while he rambled."

"So his seeing other women didn't bother you?"

"Not one bit. As I said, it was business for me. But the minute he threatened me, I ended it. He never admitted to having financial problems, but hounding me for a cut of the proceeds from my OF account when he's the owner of a successful company? That's very telling. He was a scumbag anyway."

"If you made so much money with him, why stop the gravy train with this scumbag?"

"In my line of work, men are like props. Errol fit the part: good looking, nice body, and he could perform on camera when I needed him. Sometimes we have to stop to change the camera or fix the lighting. I need someone who can stop and go. But like I said, I won't let someone strong-arm me, and he was easily replaceable."

"We appreciate you taking the time to answer our questions. It was helpful."

"You're welcome. If you have follow-up questions, you know where to find me."

Chapter Fifty-One

Jill

ALAN HEADED into the office shortly after dropping Ollie and me off at home. Ollie spent the entire time in his room, only coming out for lunch. I was content to do chores around the house to keep my mind occupied. I took a break and switched on the television, only to find breaking news airing.

SFPD had made an arrest in the Errol Tiller case. It was Helen.

I turned up the volume. The news was airing footage of Helen being transferred from a squad car into the station. She had her head down and turned away from the cameras. I couldn't believe what I was seeing.

This is impossible. Helen didn't do anything wrong.

I sat there, motionless, unable to move as I watched the horror unfold.

"If you're just tuning in, Helen Carr, a native New Yorker who moved to San Francisco only two years ago, has been arrested in connection with the death of Errol Tiller, a prominent business owner in San Francisco," said the anchorwoman. "Early Saturday morning, Mr. Tiller fell from his penthouse suite at the Residence building. It was initially thought that Mr.

Tiller had committed suicide, shocking family, friends and colleagues."

What friends? What family? No one has been in that apartment since his death except the police.

"Ms. Carr was taken into custody just minutes ago. The charges against her have not been made public, but one thing is clear: SFPD believes she is responsible for Mr. Tiller's death."

But she's innocent. I know she is!

I grabbed my phone.

"Alan, did you hear? Helen's been arrested."

"When?"

"Just now. It's breaking news. They think she killed Errol."

"Did they say why they think that?"

"No, only that the police think it's her. They aired footage of Helen walking into the station in handcuffs, like a common criminal. Helen makes candles, for God's sake! Even though that creep probably deserved it, she doesn't push people off buildings."

"Jill, I understand your frustration. I didn't like the guy either, but—"

"We have to help her, Alan. She's innocent. You know that as well as I do."

Alan paused just a little bit too long.

"You don't believe it, do you, Alan?"

"Jill, what do you want me to say? She sort of does have motive, and she had the key to his apartment."

"For crying out loud, Alan. You know Helen. She's been to the house more times than I can count."

"I know, but we don't know what the police know. We only know what Helen has told us."

"I don't care. We have to help her. Call your lawyer friend and see if he can get her out on bail, or at least be there when she's being questioned. They're probably grilling her right now."

"All right, all right. I'll call Larry."

The broadcast continued to play the footage of Helen being walked into the station. I felt so sorry for her. I couldn't imagine what that would be like. I was sure she felt humiliated, but I knew Helen was strong. She wouldn't let any of this get her down.

Alan called back ten minutes later. Larry was on his way down to the police station and had already requested the police to stop questioning Helen until he got there.

I breathed a tiny sigh of relief. I felt so helpless at that moment —even though, in the last few days, I'd had selfish thoughts about Helen's situation. I had purposely withheld information from her to protect my family's interests. If I could do that to my best friend, what did that say about me? What kind of person did that make me? A hypocrite? A selfish bitch? A backstabber?

I wanted to go to the police station, but Alan said Larry had the situation under control. Plus, the police wouldn't let me see Helen anyway. Every ten minutes, I would fire off a text message to Alan asking if he'd heard anything, and he would reply, simply: "No."

After three hours and endless "Nos," Alan finally called with news.

"Okay, here's what's happening. Larry spoke with Helen. She's doing fine. The police have arrested her on suspicion of murder, but they haven't officially charged her with anything yet. According to Larry, whatever it is, they know it's not enough, and they're hoping an arrest will scare her and make her talk."

"So what's happening now?"

"They've been interviewing Helen. They took a break, which is why Larry called, but the police can legally hold Helen for forty-eight hours without charging her. If no charges are filed, they have to release her. If she is charged, she'll remain until a preliminary hearing, where Larry will ask the judge to release Helen on bail."

"So she could be there for days?"

"She could, but Larry will do everything he can to avoid that."

I felt terrible after my call with Alan, and I also felt guilty. I had nothing to do with Helen's actions, but I somehow thought my withholding information from her must have led to the arrest. I knew it wasn't the case, but it didn't make me feel any better. Of course, there was some reassurance that Ollie's involvement would continue to diminish. Helen's arrest certainly dimmed the spotlight on our family.

I thought about the evidence against Helen: the relationship between her and Errol, the threatening emails, the demands for money...none of it looked good. I could see why the police brought her in on suspicion of murder. I wondered if they knew Helen had a key to Errol's apartment. Was that the straw that broke the camel's back? Did Peggy notify the police about the key?

Trust the process, Jill. Trust Larry.

That was all I could do at the moment.

I was in the middle of making dinner when Alan arrived home from work. I hadn't heard from him since our last conversation and was eager for an update. I stopped listening to the news for information, because it was clear they thought—or at least wanted to think—Helen was guilty of murder, and that wasn't helping my state of mind. Plus, all they did was rehash the same information over and over.

"Hi, honey," Alan said, leaning over to give me a kiss. "Where are the kids? Upstairs?"

"Yeah. Do you know anything else?"

"I spoke to Larry on the drive back home. After speaking to the detectives and the San Francisco prosecutor, he's confident the police will release Helen within an hour. It's exactly what he thought it was: a fishing expedition. They have nothing and were hoping to discover something."

"That's such a relief," I said as my shoulders dropped and I leaned my head into Alan's chest. "Will Larry take Helen home right after she's released?"

"That's the plan."

"I have to go see her. She'll need me."

"I'll hold down the fort here. What are you making?" Alan lifted the cover off the pot. "Ooh, chili? My favorite."

"I want to shower and get ready for Helen. Can you take over here?"

"Sure. On your way up, tell the kids to come downstairs."

By the time I was showered and changed, Alan had gotten word from Larry that Helen was released and he would drop her off at her apartment.

"That's wonderful news," I said. "Okay, I'm leaving now. I'm not sure when I'll be back."

"Take your time."

I hurried out the door and called Helen's phone on the drive over.

"Jill!" she answered.

"Helen, I'm on the way. I'll be there in three minutes."

Chapter Fifty-Two

Jill

HELEN HAD TOLD me to call her once I parked, and she would come down and get me. She said news vans were parked out front, and she didn't want to wait in the lobby for me. I did what she asked and hurried past the reporters. But as soon as I spotted her, so did they. Helen propped open the door.

"Hurry, Jill!" she called out.

I ran inside, slamming the door in a reporter's face.

"Sheesh, Helen. I can't believe this media circus." I gave her a huge hug. "How are you doing?"

"I'm okay, considering I was just perp walked into jail and interrogated like a murderer."

"But you're out now, and that's what matters."

We quickly made our way to the safety of Helen's apartment. Once inside, we sat on her sofa, and she told me what had happened.

"I had just returned from running a few errands when those two detectives approached me, just as I walked into the lobby. They told me I was under arrest and slapped handcuffs on me while they read me my rights. I kept thinking, 'This has to be a sick joke, and at any minute, they'll take the handcuffs off.' But they didn't. They took me right in to the station and had me sit in an interview room by myself for what must have been an hour. And at that point, they still hadn't told me anything or answered my questions. All I knew was that I'd been arrested for the murder of Errol Tiller."

"Oh, Helen, I'm sorry you had to go through this. I can't even imagine."

"Well, I want to thank you and Alan for helping. That lawyer, Larry, is an angel. I probably would have incriminated myself somehow if it wasn't for him handling those two detectives."

"So what was the reason for the arrest? Did they find out you had the key to Errol's apartment?"

"That's exactly it. I had no choice but to come clean with them and tell them about it. I said I simply forgot and didn't realize until I saw that it was missing. And yes, I mentioned I thought someone had taken it from my apartment. I named Peggy as the culprit."

"What did they say about that?"

"Nothing."

"Peggy had to have told them. Maybe she has an immunity deal or something, and that's why she's not in trouble for entering your apartment and stealing from you."

"That's what I thought, but they don't have the key."

"Wait, I'm confused. If Peggy went to them with the key, they should have it."

"It wasn't her. Someone called in an anonymous tip."

"No way. They went on some stranger's word? That's so stupid."

"That's what Larry said. They thought I would cave and confess if they could grill me and talk about this key. They didn't think they needed the key or to confirm if it even existed."

"They were bluffing."

"Yeah, and it's a good thing Larry was there. But now they know about the key, because I admitted to it."

"But wouldn't that help their case?"

"You'd think, but Larry grilled them right back. He was like, 'Unless you have evidence that places my client in that apartment when Errol went over the railing, you got nothing. Release my client.'"

"So it was all hinging on a confession," I said.

"Which I didn't give them."

"Even with you admitting you had a key to Errol's apartment, and the threats in the emails?"

"Yeah, because they have no evidence that places me in that apartment when Errol fell. And the prosecutor agreed. According to Larry, he was the one who said to cut me loose."

"So you're in the clear?"

"I am. Thank God."

I threw my arms around Helen. "I'm so happy to hear that! I really am. It just sucks that you had to go through all this to prove you didn't do anything."

"I know, but that's the game."

Helen gave me a look.

"I already know what you're about to say," I said. "Ollie isn't in the clear. There's a chance they might pull this fishing expedition with him."

"Exactly. But listen to Larry. That guy is tough. He won't let anything happen to Ollie. And plus, they have to prove Ollie was in that apartment. He was away camping."

"That's true. And Larry said there's no proof that Ollie had anything to do with the emails Grant sent to Errol."

"I don't think you have anything to worry about."

"I still can't believe that the police are willing to drag people through the mud like this."

"Me neither, but I'm guessing it produces confessions."

"So do you think they'll arrest Peggy for breaking and entering? I bet she thought she was clever calling in an anonymous tip."

"According to Larry, I'm cleared, even with admitting I had the key. There's no reason for them to follow up."

"But she broke into your apartment."

"The only proof I had was her perfume, which I can no longer smell. Even if I file an official report and they investigate, there's still no proof she was in my apartment, even if she has the key. She can just say the key is a spare. And she'd be in the right to keep spare keys; she's the building manager."

"She's getting away with it."

"Yup."

"What a conniving person. You know, I never did like her," I said.

"Not many people in the building do."

"So, what's next?" I asked.

"I no longer have to carry this weight, and I can get on with my life."

I wasn't sure what would happen with the investigation and Ollie, but I was glad Helen was no longer a part of it. Just then, my phone buzzed. Alan was calling.

"Are you still at Helen's?"

"Yeah, why?"

"Don't ask questions, just turn on the news."

I looked at Helen. "It's Alan. He wants us to watch the news."

Helen grabbed the remote and turned on the television. There was more breaking news about the Errol Tiller investigation. Now, Kelly and Grant Walker were being taken into custody.

Chapter Fifty-Three

Darrel

My wife wasn't thrilled about me going out at night. She couldn't understand why I had to meet with my boss at ten.

"Can't you talk to Ray tomorrow at work?" she'd asked as I pulled on my jacket.

"I can't. This conversation has to happen tonight. I'll explain everything to you when I come home." I kissed her goodbye and left.

Ray had called me an hour ago and asked for the meeting. Usually, I would tell him to save it until work the next day, but the current circumstances called for the meeting. We always met at a small bar in the Outer Sunset District; Ray lived nearby.

Ray was already there when I arrived, sitting in a booth toward the back of the place. He had his usual drink, bourbon. I acknowledged him on the way to the bar to grab a beer. A few moments later, I slid into the booth.

"You're on time," he said.

"I know. I told you I'd get better. Is he on his way?"

"Yeah, I just got a text from him. He should be here soon."

"Is he still bitching about meeting over here?"

"He is." Ray took a sip of his bourbon.

"Man, he shouldn't be complaining. He might be paying us, but we're also doing him a favor."

"There he is," Ray said.

Near the door, I saw Ross Meyer, Peggy's husband, looking lost. I waved my arm until he spotted us.

"We sit at the same table every time," I muttered to Ray. "Can't he remember?"

"Hey, guys. Sorry I'm late. It's a long drive from Tiburon, and I don't have much time. What's the latest with my wife?"

Ross had approached Ray and me about four months ago. He thought his wife might be cheating on him and asked us if we could keep an eye on her—for a fee, of course. It was good money, so Ray and I agreed. We figured nothing would come of it, because Ross thought it was some guy who worked in the Financial District. He wanted us to keep track of the men coming to meet Peggy at her office. Turned out, she was screwing Mr. Tiller.

It was really easy to keep an eye on her after that. I even gave Ross footage of his wife leaving Mr. Tiller's apartment. Ross was collecting all this stuff so he could divorce Peggy and not have to pay up. There was some wording in the prenup that she would still get a certain amount of money if the divorce were amicable, so he wanted proof that his wife was cheating.

"Peggy did some screwed-up stuff," I said. "She used her keys to break into a resident's apartment."

"She what? Why?"

"She's getting all paranoid about Mr. Tiller's death. She thinks the police will eventually tell you about them if they keep investigating, so she's trying to make it go away."

"I already know about her cheating. So how does breaking into an apartment get rid of the cops?"

"The apartment she broke into belonged to Helen Carr. She was also seeing Mr. Tiller."

"Wait, isn't that the woman who was arrested today?" Ross asked.

"Yeah, that's her. They released her, though."

"That's weird."

"I had to report what Peggy did to Ray."

"And I'm glad Darrel did, because I took it up with the owner of the building."

"And?"

"He's firing Peggy tomorrow. I'll move into her position as the new building manager. And Darrel here will take my old position."

"I can't believe it. Not only is she getting canned, but she's also getting served. I'm supposed to have the papers ready tomorrow."

"One more thing you should know," Ray said. "She told Darrel she found a key in Ms. Carr's apartment that goes to Mr. Tiller's. We don't know what's going on with this key and why it was so important for her to take it, but I couldn't let it slide. If it was connected to the investigation of Mr. Tiller's death, I had to report it."

"You told the police?"

"I made an anonymous tip. It seemed to make a difference at first, because they arrested Ms. Carr, but then they let her go. Don't know why."

"Well, I don't care about that other stuff unless it helps build my case when she comes for the money. I appreciate all the help, and congratulations on the promotions."

Ross left as quickly as he came.

"Man, Peggy is about to have one hell of a day tomorrow," I said.

"She sure is."

"You see this?" I said, pointing to one of the televisions over the bar. "First, they arrest Ms. Carr, and now the police are taking in Mrs. Walker and her son? It's crazy."

"Well, they already released Ms. Carr. They might do the same with those two. Who knows? We might already know what happened if Peggy had installed security cameras like I told her to."

"No doubt about that."

"There'll be a lot of changes at the Residence. I think the folks that live there will appreciate it."

"For sure."

"Oh, and Darrel—don't ever deal drugs there again. Don't think I didn't pick up on that."

I held up my hands. "It'll never happen again. You and me, we cool."

Chapter Fifty Four

Jill

It was Saturday morning, and I was on my way to meet Helen at the farmers' market. I was looking forward to the return of my weekly meetups with her at the Ferry Building. The drama of the past week had taken its toll on my family. I still couldn't get over what happened.

When Helen and I had watched Kelly and her son get dragged into the station, we knew it was another witch hunt and that they would be released. We were learning that the police had a bunch of circumstantial evidence that suggested Errol might have been murdered, but that was it. They were, as Larry had put it, on a fishing expedition. Shortly after the nightly news, Kelly and Grant were released.

Ollie was eager to call his friend, and seeing they had been cleared, we let him. Through Ollie, we learned the police tried to paint Kelly and Grant as a team working together to get rid of Errol.

I thought that was absolutely insane. Grant had an alibi; he was camping with his father. And even though Kelly had admitted to visiting Errol that night, they had no proof that she had been there when Errol died—or that she pushed him.

Ollie told us that Grant's father was willing to work things out with Kelly, which made Grant happy. It was a shame that all that had to come out in the open, but as with most news, it passed, and people forgot about it.

By the following day, the news cycle had changed once again. They had returned to reporting that Errol had committed suicide, as that was how SFPD had ruled on the investigation. The financial problems at his company had also come out, and so had multiple sexual harassment complaints against him. Thankfully, Mia's name wasn't mentioned. Even Ms. Martin had spoken with the media and told them about Errol's threats to her. She had also officially retired from teaching and was no longer employed by Ollie's school. When you consider all that information, it paints a picture of a man spinning out of control.

"What a wild week," Helen said as she dug into her omelet. "I still can't believe that arrest turned out to be a good thing. My candle sales are through the roof. I'll have to hire more staff."

"What's the saying? 'Any press is good press'? I'm happy for you, Helen. You deserve it after the week you had."

"Thank you for being there for me, and for hiring that lawyer. I can't thank you and Alan enough. I'm paying back every cent he charged you. It's money well spent. How are the kids doing?"

"Mia's fine. She's a tough cookie. Ollie is just glad that he's got his friend back."

"Did Alan give him back his photography equipment?"

"He did, but with rules. Ollie swears he learned his lesson. And I believe him. I mean, what happened this week is enough drama to last a lifetime."

"Here's to forgetting this ever happened." Helen lifted her coffee cup, and I bumped mine against it.

The big question was whether Alan and I had learned our lesson. I would say yes and no. I knew Alan. I knew who he was when I got involved with him, and certainly when I agreed to marry him. He wasn't going to stop watching people, and I accepted that. Was it right for everyone? Probably not, but with Alan, it seemed to work. And I *did* enjoy watching the Mortons bicker at night.

We'd since agreed to put our peeping on pause. No set time limit. I hoped we would discover another hobby he and I could enjoy together.

Chapter Fifty-Five

Alan

IT WAS ANOTHER RELAXING WEEKEND. Ollie had left the house to hang out with Grant, Mia was out with her friends, and Jill was at her weekly meetup with Helen. I had the place all to myself. Usually, I would have relished the peace and quiet, choosing to watch TV and snack on a big bag of chips. But that Saturday morning, I felt antsy, so I walked to the nearby dog park to watch the dogs play with each other. It wasn't just people I liked to watch. Dogs were fantastic subjects.

I took a seat on a bench and stretched my legs out. The skies were clear, the air crisp and fresh. I watched a little terrier play with a German Shepherd. It was an odd pairing, but they appeared to be great friends.

"Hello, Mr. Pittman."

I looked away from the dogs and found Geneva Garrett standing a few feet away. She was a sixteen-year-old who lived in the Residence with her mother.

"Hi, Geneva. It's been a while."

"It has."

"How are things?"

"I'm fine. It's a beautiful morning. I thought I'd bring Mr. Silly to the park."

I reached my hand out so the pug could catch my scent. After a sniff or two, he began licking my hand. "Yeah, boy. You remember me, right?"

"So, Mr. Silly, huh?" I said as I looked up at Geneva.

"I know. But I couldn't bring myself to call him Mr. Tiller."

Not many people knew Geneva had been hired to walk Errol's dog. She was a quiet girl who tended to blend in with her surroundings. She really seemed to enjoy her time with the pug. About two and a half weeks ago, Errol had given Geneva his dog. He'd told her the pug liked her more, anyway.

"When I would walk him, I would call him 'Mr. Silly' because it sounded a little close to 'Mr. Tiller,'" she said. "He always responded, so when he became mine, I made the name change official."

"Well, I think that's a perfect name. He is a silly little dog."

I'd initially met Geneva through Mia. I'd never heard Mia mention her before, even though they went to the same school and were in the same grade. She said Geneva was super quiet and always hung out in the library.

One day, Mia joined me on a walk to the dog park and confided in me. She'd come across Geneva crying in the school bathroom. Mia said it took a bit of prodding before Geneva told her what was happening to her: Errol had been sexually assaulting her ever since she started walking his dog. My immediate concern was for Geneva's safety. We had to involve the authorities—and inform Geneva's mother. Mia protested that we couldn't go to the police, *because* Geneva didn't want her mom to know.

Geneva had lost her father two years ago. According to Geneva, her mother never quite recovered from his sudden death. She was constantly depressed. Geneva believed something like this could drive her mother to take her own life.

"Why are you telling me this, Mia?" I'd asked her. "I'm glad you came to me, but why not your mom?"

"I can't tell mom; she'll just freak out. But you're different. I know you can figure out a way we can help Geneva."

Shortly after our conversation, I'd come up with a solution.

That was the day I began paying closer attention to Errol. Geneva would always go to his apartment in the afternoons to take the dog for a walk. Since I was at work, I'd always set up my telescope to record around that time. I learned that Errol had also given her a key to his apartment, as he wasn't home most afternoons unless it was a weekend. But even on weekends, he still had Geneva come up and walk the pug.

One day, I caught the two in his apartment embracing each other. It wasn't a platonic greeting; I knew what that looked like. This was an intimate hug. And I didn't think it was the type of scenario where Geneva had a naive crush on Errol and had finally acted on it. So what Mia had told me so far was true.

What I soon discovered from my watching was that every Saturday Errol and Geneva would disappear into his bedroom. According to Mia, that's when he would have sex with her. My plan was to catch him in the act and turn my recording over to the police—even though Geneva didn't want that, I couldn't stand by and do nothing. Mia also said Errol had told Geneva that if she didn't continue spending time with him, he would hurt her mother. Geneva had made the mistake of telling Errol that her mother was mentally unstable, and that bastard used it against her.

Hearing this made my blood boil. I wanted to beat the crap out of Errol. But I knew that wasn't the way to go. And what made things worse was not being able to capture the footage I wanted to make it a slam dunk rape case. In all my years of watching, I never thought I'd be looking for something like this. I asked Mia if Geneva would meet with me. I needed to hear everything from her.

During our conversation at the dog park, Geneva begged me not to tell her mother, the police, or anyone for that matter. But I couldn't let it continue. Errol had to be stopped. And then Geneva dropped the bombshell. Errol had gotten her pregnant.

In California, minors do not need parental permission to obtain an abortion. Geneva didn't want to keep Errol's baby, and Mia had already agreed to go with Geneva to the clinic.

But as far as I was concerned, that wasn't the end of the story. I had a plan to deal with Errol.

One thing I will tell you about watching people is that you learn a lot about their routines the longer you watch them.

I learned Errol was having sex with two women in the building: Kelly Walker and Peggy Meyer. Yes, I knew about their affairs long before anyone else did. I also knew Errol was a raging cokehead and most likely a high-functioning alcoholic. I knew Darrel Knight supplied his coke. I knew Helen was a dominatrix who liked to whip Errol. I knew Ms. Ezra was always on her balcony, trying to listen in on Errol's business. I knew that enough people in the building had a connection to Errol that his death would create a real-life whodunit.

I actively recruited Errol to bring his business to my firm, just so I could get a peek into his financials. He was in serious debt, and while he was asset rich, he was cash poor. And the partners at his firm were set on ousting him. That's a lot of failure for a narcissistic person to take. It could even drive him to take his own life. No one would suspect otherwise. It was simply a matter of covering my tracks.

The emails that Jill found on my computer were dummy

emails. I had set them up in case she ever found out Errol was a client. I also intended for her to find my photo cache. She needed to. I wanted to minimize the backlash when she found out her son was also watching. And she would. Ollie and I planned it that way.

When Ollie was four, I began to suspect he was like me. He would sit still and stare at people, studying them, and later recall details. When Ollie was old enough, I told him how his mother and I met. He thought it was neat.

I needed Ollie on board if I was going to pull off the plan with Errol. I took what I knew and built a plan, starting with informing Grant about his mother. Of course, he was devastated, but Ollie made sure Grant knew there was a way to get back at Errol if he listened to me. With Grant on board, we could get the plan rolling. So long as Ollie and Grant played their parts—Grant as the angry teen and Ollie as the horndog teen—I would be able to get to Errol.

Helen was the other part of my plan. I knew from watching that Helen had a key to Errol's apartment. I needed access. It just so happened that when I approached her to feel her out, she told me about the deal she had with Errol. I mentioned what he had done to Geneva, and that was all she'd needed to hear to come on board.

So I had my team in place: Ollie, Grant, and Helen. I'd decided to leave Mia out of it. Everyone else who would get caught up in Errol's death, like Peggy and Kelly, could carry on with whatever they were doing. I was confident none of them, or anyone on my team, would be found guilty of murder. But there would be just enough suspicion cast on everyone that I could be a wolf in sheep's clothing and gain access to Errol's apartment that night.

Everything worked as planned—except for one thing. I

never suspected Jill would look through my telescope at the exact moment I threw Errol off his balcony. What were the odds? But luck favored me that night. Jill had drunk two bottles of wine and wasn't entirely sure what she had seen.

As for Geneva, she had no idea what my team and I had done. She thought Errol gave her the dog because he planned on committing suicide. That worked for me.

No doubt, there had been some stressful moments, but I told everyone involved that justice would prevail if they kept the faith. And I believed it. So did Helen and Grant, even when they were arrested. Everything worked out just like I thought it would.

Kent sticking by Kelly was a pleasant surprise. Grant was thrilled, as were Ollie and I. Kelly was a good person who'd made a mistake. She deserved a second chance.

Peggy was the only person who ended up with the short end of the stick in all of this, but she had dug herself into that hole. She was let go by the owner of the building, and her husband did serve her divorce papers. Their divorce was the talk of the town as they squabbled over her husband's wealth. She managed to get some money from him, but not the level she had expected or hoped for. Last I heard, she had plans to move away from the Bay Area. I doubted many people would miss her.

My team and I kept in touch through a secret chat group I had set up. We had all taken on aliases from the Astro Boy comic. I was Astro Boy, Ollie was Jetto, Helen was Astro Girl, and Grant had chosen Professor Ochanomizu.

Before deleting the group chat, I thanked my team and told them never to mention our actions to anyone. We had done our jobs, and it was over. Time to forget it all.

"Enjoy the rest of your day, Mr. Pittman," Geneva said as she led Mr. Silly away.

258258

"I will. You enjoy yours as well."

I knew two wrongs didn't make a right, but I also saw the world as a better place without Errol Tiller. Who knew? Errol might have jumped one day with how things were playing out. As much as I thought watching was a good thing, that would be the one time I simply did not want to watch and see.

Epilogue

Jill

I'M the woman who spotted you in the dark woods through my dorm room window. That shadowy image of you is seared into my memory. I can pick you out of any dark environment. You'd be wrong to think otherwise. I may have finished two bottles of wine that Friday night, but I'm no lush. Sara, my college roommate, taught me how to hold my liquor. Do I need to know the details? No, I do not. Errol was a bastard and deserved what was coming to him. I'll never forget what he did to our daughter.

Yes, Alan Pittman, I saw you on that balcony. Because I've become a watcher just like you.

Click to read It Ends Now. Addie Baxley ran away from her hometown when she was eighteen. Twelve years later, she came back. So has the terror.

A Note from Ty Hutchinson

Thank you for reading THE VIEW FROM NOB HILL. If you're a fan, spread the word to friends, family, book clubs, and reader groups online. You can also help get the word out by leaving a review.

Sign up for my Spam-Free Newsletter to receive "First Look" content, and information about future releases and giveaways.

I love hearing from readers. Let's connect.
www.tyhutchinson.com
tyhutchinson@tyhutchinson.com

Also by Ty Hutchinson

Abby Kane FBI Thrillers

Corktown

Tenderloin

Russian Hill (CC Trilogy #1)

Lumpini Park (CC Trilogy #2)

Coit Tower (CC Trilogy #3)

Kowloon Bay

Suitcase Girl (SG Trilogy #1)

The Curator (SG Trilogy #2)

The Hatchery (SG Trilogy #3)

Find Yuri (Fury Trilogy #1)

Crooked City (Fury Trilogy #2)

Good Bad Psycho (Fury Trilogy #3)

The Puzzle Maker

The Muzzle Job

Fire Catcher

Psychological Thrillers

The View from Nob Hill

It Ends Now

The Friend Group

Mui Action Thrillers

The Monastery

The Blood Grove

The Minotaur

Darby Stansfield Thrillers

The Accidental Criminal

(previously titled Chop Suey)

The Russian Problem

(previously titled Stroganov)

Holiday With A P.I.

(previously titled Loco Moco)

Darby Stansfield Box Set

Other Thrilling Reads

The Perfect Plan

The St. Petersburg Confession

Published by Ty Hutchinson

Copyright © 2023 by Ty Hutchinson

Cover Art: Damonza

Made in the USA
Las Vegas, NV
10 March 2024

86975619R00156